LIVING TO DIE

Russell D Whitney

WOW Book Publishing™

Thanks to Vishal and team at
Wow Publishing Ltd and to Bernice Filippou.

Acknowledgements

This is my first book and I sincerely hope it will not be my last. I would like to dedicate this work to my partner, Sarah HG.

Sarah is the one who said "you can" rather than "you could". She has allowed me the time and space to be creative and has supported me unconditionally.

With the right person behind you, anything is possible. God bless Mum and Dad.

Russell D Whitney

To follow Russell and the latest news on his books follow him on Facebook and Instagram

Instagram @Russell.Whitney.1 Facebook @Russellsbooks

E-Mail Russellsbooks1@gmail.com

LIVING TO DIE

We all dream; sometimes, the dreams seem incredibly real. That's fine if it's a nice dream, but what if it's a nightmare?

What makes it a nightmare?

Is it something you are afraid of, or is it something lurking in your subconscious?

What if it's the nasty dreams, the nightmares that come true?

Would you be afraid to sleep if your dreams became worse?

What would be worse than seeing some- one you know die?

Chapter 1

Although they went to school together, Steve had never spoken to Sally. He had always liked her, but, like so many boys his age, he was shy when it came to talking to girls; he asked his best friend, Neil, to ask her out for him. A huge mistake. She became Neil's girlfriend for two tortuous weeks.

Steve thought his heart would be broken forever the day he looked out of his bedroom window to see the two of them riding past on a new Raleigh Chopper bicycle.

Thankfully, Neil's attention span was very short, and, as soon as Christine Parsons moved to the area, he lost interest in Sally. Steve was the first to console her, and, after what seemed an absolute age, he won her over.

Their romance lasted a blissful eleven days, fourteen hours, twenty-seven minutes, and three seconds until she dumped him for an older boy with a new moped.

Steve and Sally had met for the second time through a mutual friend, Sandra. It was Sandra's 22nd birthday party, and she decided to invite some of her old school friends, including Steve and Sally.

The party was one to remember; not only had Sally turned up, she seemed very pleased to see him and was blatantly flirting. She spent most of the evening taking pictures with her new camera; photography had always been a huge passion. This time, Steve knew he had to take the lead, to be a little more forceful in the romance game, and it paid off.

Sally had been to university, studying law; she was always a step ahead of her peers, and, when her other friends were dancing until 2am, Sally was studying hard. She did very well, gaining a degree with honours. Steve didn't understand how much she had put into her education; unfortunately, he regarded school as a place to socialise and was more interested in earning money to fix up his motorbike.

Both Steve and Sally had not kept in touch with many of their school friends, so it was nice to see some of them again. Alan, who had followed his father's footsteps in the haulage business, was one of those they hadn't seen in years.

By the time he was twenty, he had managed to buy his first truck. With the help of his family, lots of hard work, and determination, he had successfully acquired a fleet of vehicles and two haulage yards. His business was turning over millions of pounds a year.

The music was so loud it made any conversation difficult. Despite being tired, Steve was on an emotional high; he and Sally had kissed at last, and he was on cloud nine. Before she left, she promised to meet him the following day.

Chapter 2

Sandra woke early; she was unexpectedly alone. As she walked into her living room, she realized that she had no idea inviting thirty people into a small, two-bedroom apartment would cause such a mess.

She sat naked at the breakfast bar, drinking a cup of Fazenda Santas Ines coffee, one of her many indulgences (like Fleur du Mal silk lingerie and chocolate chilli vodka). She had no concept of money and how much she spent on her luxuries; luckily for her, she had an allowance from Daddy every month. She had no idea where the money came from and tried not to think about it too much.

Thankfully, she had the whole day off. As a nurse, she worked ridiculous hours, and this was her first day off in eleven days. She promised herself that as soon as everything was back to her idea of "tidy", she would go back to bed. She also hoped it wouldn't be on her own.

Sandra had quite a reputation around the hospital; she knew what her fellow nurses thought, but she didn't give a shit. As far as she was concerned, she had one life, and she liked to live it to the fullest. She went into the bathroom, sat on the toilet, and noticed her knickers on top of the bathroom cabinet; she sniggered even more as she tried to remember how they got there.

She reached up to get them, only to find two pairs. She laughed to herself even more and decided she should have a party more often. A moment later, the doorbell rang. Picking up her dressing gown from the floor and putting it on, she answered the door. Her face lit up when she saw it was Sally; she had a wicked smile on her face and was holding her camera.

Chapter 3

Steve's morning was not great. He woke up just after mid-day and had a hangover like none before. All he could think about was Sally.

Then he realized he had no idea where they said they were going to meet. He checked his pockets to see if he had written her number down. Nothing. Panic struck him; he felt even sicker than when he woke and could smell the unmistakable odour of Pernod in his room, which made him feel worse.

He sat on the edge of his bed staring into space for ages then heard the sound of the landline ringing downstairs. He heard his mum, who always raised her voice on the phone to make sure deaf people could hear her.

He heard her repeatedly asking, "Who are you?" and "Yes dear, no dear". Steve pulled his pyjama bottoms on and rushed downstairs just as his mother put the phone down.

Thankfully, Sally phoned back an hour later. When she arrived in her car later that afternoon to pick him up, Steve's day got even better.

The moment he saw her, he had palpitations. She looked and smelled amazing, and, as far as he was concerned, nothing else mattered if they were together.

They went to the local park where they sat in the car while Sally took pictures of the swans on the lake. Rain lashed down. It was probably just as well; it helped give the two of them some privacy.

The windows misted up from the body heat in the car; even the most persistent voyeur would have had trouble seeing the serious petting going on. Steve was quite shocked in how forward Sally was; he was surprised when she started to rub the bulge in his jeans and almost choked when she slid her hand inside them.

Chapter 4

Steve had never been ambitious; after leaving school, he went to the local technical college and studied automotive engineering with the intent of becoming a mechanic like his late father.

Most of Steve's friends, equally lacking in ambition, ended up in a similar industry as their fathers, and most of them seemed happy with their choice.

Eventually, a job came up at the Ford dealership close to where Steve lived. He applied for it, and after a brief interview with the Dealer Principal Keith Higgins, he was offered the job.

It was tough being the apprentice; he was the butt of all the jokes for the first few weeks. On his first day, his mentor told him to go ask for a long stand at the parts department. A man in dirty overalls asked him to wait outside the back entrance for a moment. Being naïve, Steve waited an hour before asking the man where his long stand was. The man laughed and told him to go back to the workshop; he had been standing long enough.

Thankfully, it didn't take too long to realise he was being made a fool. He understood it was all in the name of good fun and was all part of the learning curve.

One thing Steve liked was stability in his life; he loved routine. He would wake up the same time every day. You could even set a watch by his bathroom routine. 6am: have a pee; wash his face with cold water. Make a cup of tea at 6:10 and a bowl of cornflakes with brown sugar. 6:31am: sit on the loo, let nature take its course, and shave with his trusted electric shaver at the same time ("time in motion" he called it).

There was only one thing he loathed: mobile phones. He vowed never to have one; this reluctance to embrace modern technology was more of a problem for people trying to contact him rather than the other way around.

His stability collapsed when his mother died; it was a huge shock for everyone as she showed no signs of being ill. Two weeks after her diagnosis, she died.

He didn't want to continue living in the house and decided to rent a small studio apartment down the road.

It was a huge step to take, but, with Sally's support, he managed to get a level of stability back. It also meant Sally could stay with him more often.

The dreams were always there and very vivid. From a young age, he used to get reoccurring dreams; one of them was related to his fear of heights.

There was a footbridge close to Steve's school known as the Curly Wurly Bridge because of its 360-degree spiral that lead to the highest point of 5.02 metres.

On any day, you could stand on the bridge and feel it bounce, especially if a large truck went under it.

The dream was that he was lying on top of the bridge, peering down at the traffic passing under him. He was convinced he was going to fall; completely illogical, but you tend not to think of dreams in a logical way while you are having them.

This was one of the dreams that would wake him suddenly. He didn't dream every night; in fact, in his youth, not much thought went into his dreaming. There were few he remembered. On a couple of occasions, while going through puberty, he woke to find the bed was wet. This was an interesting time in his life as he began to think about what the other boys called "sexy things".

Sally and Steve saw each other every day without fail, and it wasn't long before they started talking about the future.

Sally had secured a job with a new group of lawyers in the local town of Christchurch, and it wasn't long before she was well respected. She was earning good money, and the two of them decided to look for a place of their own.

Sadly, Sally's mother, Patricia, had been ill for a while and had to go into a nursing home. She was suffering from dementia, having showed signs of it from an early age. This was a terrible strain overall, and, as she became worse, the visits became more stressful.

Sally's father, Robert, was amazing; he understood exactly what was going on and was taking everything in his stride.

He was a renowned lawyer and had done extremely well. He had a reputation of being the kind of person people shouldn't mess with. Apparently, if you were very naughty but extremely wealthy, this was the man you wanted on your side.

Steve thought he was great, especially because Robert kept a collection of classic cars and motorcycles inside his huge bespoke garage.

The motorcycle collection was of a lot more interesting to Steve; not many people owned two Vincent Black Lightning's. Work was the same for Steve.

Every day, he would turn up and get the job done. He was popular at work and had the reputation of being a first-class mechanic. It soon became apparent that he had wasted his secondary education but had become very keen to improve his skills. The garage also wanted him to improve; he attended a number of courses, and it wasn't long before he was entered in a competition for technician of the year.

The final was to be held in Spain; it consisted of several theory and practical tests over a three-day period. Steve studied books, graphs, and even stayed late at work one night to rebuild a gearbox blindfolded. He did it with ease, except for stripping a bolt, which he had never done before.

The day before flying out to Spain, Steve and Sally looked at a house, a lovely new build with three bedrooms and bathrooms with a garage for the bike.

Sally could turn the small room into a dark room, and it was only twenty minutes from the garage. Sally's father was going to pay the deposit for them, but they had to do the adult thing and get a mortgage. Life was good.

Sally used to stay at Steve's small apartment quite often. The night before the flight, she stayed at home; Steve needed to get up at 4am to get to Southampton Airport. He was due in Valencia for an afternoon meeting with his examiner and the other competitors.

Chapter 5

Dean was one of Steve's colleagues at the Ford Dealership. He worked in the parts department and had been there for fifteen years. No one knew much about him, except that he lived with his mother in the house he was born in. As far as his colleagues were concerned, Dean was very much a loner.

He cycled to work every day, because he said it kept him. However, cycling less than a mile to work probably did little for his fitness. He was one of those lucky people who had the type of metabolism that kept him thin.

He had been supporting his mother since his father suffered a massive stroke and died. Dean and his mother were thankful he had passed quickly; his father was so independent, fit, and ironically healthy, he would have hated to have been reliant on anyone, especially his son.

All Dean's mother ever wanted was for him to find a wife, marry, and have children.

What she saw was a rake of a man who went to work every day with jam sandwiches, ready salted crisps, two wafer bars, and a can of fizzy orange.

He would be at home at 6:30 pm and have his dinner, already sitting on the table for him when he got in. At 7:45 pm, Dean would leave the house to go and play darts in The George, their local pub. At least, that's what his mother thought. He did play darts but only until 9 pm. Afterwards, he visited his lady friend who lived opposite the pub; her husband worked nights.

Chapter 6

Steve threw the covers off; he was soaked. Shaking, he looked at the clock.

It was 12:03 am.

Dazed and confused, he looked at the clock again. Totally disorientated, he looked around the room, sat on the side of the bed, and tried to get his bearings. "That was must have been some dream," he thought, because he couldn't remember a thing about it.

He went to the bathroom, washed his face, went to the toilet and climbed back into bed. Now wide- awake, he lay there for what seemed ages before he eventually fell asleep. His alarm rang at 3 am.

Even at 3am, the routine was the same: shit, shave, and shower. He was ready at 4 am for Clive to pick him up, his chaperone for the trip. Clive was an Independent Service Manager who looked after trainees and was chosen to go with Steve at the last moment.

Steve opened the door and stepped out into the cold, misty, murky morning.

He quietly closed the front door and turned around; he was shocked to see Sally standing in front of him.

"What the hell are you doing here?" he asked. He then saw Sally's face; she was sobbing uncontrollably.

"Mum's dead", Sally said.

"She died this morning; I'm sorry," she said, sobbing uncontrollably. "I had to see you.

Mum died in hospital at three minutes past twelve."

Steve froze.

Chapter 7

Clive sat in the departure lounge, looking at Steve; he felt sick, but not as sick as Steve was feeling.

Clive tried to reason with him, telling him that he should have stayed home. However, Sally insisted that Steve should go on the trip as he had put so much time and effort into preparing for the event.

Clive felt extremely uncomfortable; he was a man of little emotion, an ideal man for his job, or so he thought. The man had no people skills at all and was quite happy to get rid of an employee with issues, something Steve had already thought about. He loved his job but was now thinking what would happen to him if he screwed up.

So many things were going through his mind; as much as he tried, he couldn't remember what the dream had been about. There was no explanation of what had happened to him at 12:03 am.

The day got worse. The written exam was about a new type of ECU (Electronic Control Unit) that had regular updates and the Central Fuel Injection system. On any normal day, Steve could quote from the manual. Now, he was struggling to remember what ECU even stood for.

When it came to the practical exam again, Steve had studied exactly what he needed to and it would be quite an easy job for him (a rebuild of an automatic gearbox). Sadly, things did not go to plan at all.

Clive sat with Steve in the bar that evening, speechless. For a while, Steve thought he had found some compassion, but the man was fuming. Steve had let everyone down.

"This won't ever happen again," Clive thought to himself.

It took a while for everyone to get over Patricia's death. It turned out she had a massive heart attack. It sounds awful, but most people were relieved; it meant the family could grieve at last.

Steve kept quiet about waking up the night Patricia died; it wasn't easy. He badly wanted to talk to Sally about it but decided it wouldn't make much of a difference.

The two of them had talked about everything; there had never been secrets. They were honest with each other. Because of this, he felt guilty for not having shared what happened that night, but he put it down to sheer coincidence.

Chapter 8

Life began to fall into what Steve regarded as normality, and they moved into their lovely little new three-bedroom semi. They were the first ones to move into the close, new development of nine identical houses. Located on a no-through road, it was nice and quiet.

Work carried on the same, exactly how Steve liked it; routine was king for him. It took a long while for everyone to forgive him for messing up in Valencia, but when his co-workers found out about Sally's mother, they understood.

Sally was also very settled at work, and there was a rumour she could become a partner at the law firm. One of the existing partners was a very professional woman. Everyone called her by her surname, Billington, and she wouldn't talk to anyone who didn't address her by her name.

Every day, she wore the same thing: black patent high heels, black tights, a white blouse, a pinstripe jacket and a tie. The tie was the only thing she changed every day. The other staff thought she had over three hundred ties; they never remembered seeing the same one more than once.

Billington's auburn hair was always up, and she looked stunning. Sally had quite a crush on the woman, but that was Sally's secret. Just one more in a long line.

No one at the office had any idea of Billington's personal life; she never spoke of anything outside work, a real woman of mystery.

It was Robert who started dropping hints about weddings, and he even brought Sally a subscription to Bride Magazine to push things along.

One evening, Robert called and invited Steve and Sally to his house for a chat; he had something to talk to them about. Steve joked about Robert finally getting a lady friend.

It had been very hard for Robert all through Patricia's illness. He would go and see her every day in the care home that he preferred to call the hotel. In reality, the Presidential Suite in the Hilton would have been cheaper, but he didn't care about the money. Thankfully, that was the least of his troubles.

Some days, Patricia wouldn't even recognise him, and that hurt. He would sit by her bed for a couple of hours, but other days she never woke. Robert hoped she was dreaming of the lovely times they had together.

He missed her company as well; Patricia was such an elegant lady. She always looked her best; he had never seen her in a pair of jogging bottoms or a wrinkled old sweatshirt, let alone a pair of slippers.

The one thing that used to upset him was the time it took her to get ready for anything.

Robert worked it out once; in one year, she spent 960 hours getting ready. That's 40 days they could have spent in their beloved St. Lucia, but boy, was she worth it.

The three of them sat around the beautifully prepared dinner table. Robert had ordered a catering company, complete with a maid and butler. "A little extravagant," Sally thought. Steve loved it, especially the maid's outfit that left little to the imagination. Sally also noticed it and decided she would have a discrete chat with the young woman.

The food was amazing, home-cooked, and limitless in its options. Steve toyed with the idea of ordering fish fingers, beans, and chips. As not to upset anyone, he went for sea bass and salad. Both Sally and Robert asked for roast lamb, which was cooked to perfection.

Eventually, during the dessert course, Robert said he needed to talk to them but wanted them to listen to him before interrupting.

The first thing he told them was that he had booked a well-known castle in Dorset for their wedding. He told them he had already paid for it and gave them three dates to choose from, the first one being in two weeks. Then the other dates were in the following year.

Secondly, he was selling his car and bike collection. Steve was just about to object, but Robert stood and told them to listen. He needed to go away for a while, and he was leaving that night.

No explanation was given; he promised that when he got to his destination, he would call them.

Both Sally and Steve were aware that Robert mixed in some unfavourable circles, but, when you have some clients like Robert's, life could be unpredictable.

A few years ago, Robert got a petty criminal out on bail. The following day, the man went on to commit armed robbery. It was well publicised as he shot a security guard. Unfortunately, his getaway driver left him outside a building society with a shotgun and a holdall containing four thousand pounds. If Robert hadn't got the man out on bail, the security officer would still have two legs.

Both Steve and Sally sat in the back of the new Range Rover while being driven home; Steve went into the house and left Sally talking to her father in the car. An hour later, Sally entered the house, holding a gift box containing a new Nikon camera. Her red eyes told the rest of the story. They said nothing but goodnight and love you. They both lay in bed, trying to get some sleep. Neither of them was going to get much rest that night.

At 3:48 am, Robert boarded a private jet at Bournemouth Airport.

"No!" Steve shouted at the top of his voice.

He sat up, covered in sweat, and began shaking.

Sally was petrified; she thought there was someone in their room. She switched her alarm clock light on, turned to Steve, and grabbed him. He was shaking so much, his arms were flapping around his head. He was soaked as if someone had thrown a bucket of hot water over him.

Sally was scared, frightened he was going to hurt her. She shouted at him, called his name. Steve just sat bolt upright, his face pale, and his eyes were wide open staring in front of him.

She shouted again. "Please wake up, Steve. It's me; wake up." Sally watched as if a soul was leaving him. A few seconds later, he shook his head.

"Sally, where are you?" he asked.

She put her arms around him as he began to cry. He sobbed like a baby.

Sally reached over to get the bottle of water she kept by her bed. "Drink this sweetheart," she said. He took the bottle of water and drunk the full litre.

A few minutes later, he looked the same as he always did. "What the hell is going on Steve?" she asked. "I had a nightmare. I had a nightmare that . . . that . . ." He had no idea what had happened. "I can't remember," he repeated and began to cry again.

Sally was frightened.

Steve did fall asleep again. Sally stayed up, watching over him. Desperate for a pee, she moved as quietly as possible to the edge of the bed. She slid one leg out, before she heard him cry out,

"Don't go babe."

"I need a pee," she replied, and she swung her other leg out of the bed and walked into the bathroom.

Steve sat up in bed; he was worried about what to say to Sally, and he only had seconds to think. She walked out of the bathroom and sat on the edge of the bed next to him. A moment later, she heard something she never expected to hear.

"I'm going to take the day off work; I'll call in sick," he said.

Sally went to work but had trouble concentrating on anything. What had her father gotten himself into?

What was that all about last night?

Her mind worked overtime on all the possibilities, and she wondered if Steve was in trouble.

She almost dismissed that as soon as she thought it; how much trouble can a mechanic with OCD tendencies be in? She knew there was no chance of him having an affair; he just didn't have the time. Unlike her.

Chapter 9

"Sally? Sally", is everything ok?"

Billington was sitting in one of the classic red leather chairs in front of Sally's desk. Sally looked up and apologised for not concentrating; she looked at Billington.

Sally's mind wandered again; she was trying to imagine what was under the business suit. As if on purpose, Billington crossed her legs slowly leaving Sally no doubt about the stockings or tights underneath. This made Sally smile, and she was back in the land of the conscious.

Sally smiled again and did an imaginary punch in the air. "Results!" she thought. "Results!"

It was only a matter of time.

Chapter 10

Steve did very little all day. He tried to go back to sleep; he needed to get back to his dream. He lay in bed for ages, closing his eyes. There was no way he was going to fall asleep. He kept on thinking about the dream he had; was it a dream or a premonition?

The only time he got out of bed for the rest of the day was to have some cornflakes and a cup of tea. He even took them back to bed.

At 4:30 pm, after watching the third episode of Top Gear on TV, he jumped in the shower, had a shave, and made himself a little more presentable for when his beloved got home around 6 pm.

At 5:30 pm, the phone rang. He knew exactly what Sally was going to say; she apologised and said she would be home by 8 pm and to not worry about food; she would eat at her desk.

Steve poured himself another bowl of cornflakes, put the TV back on, and searched for the next episode of Top Gear.

Chapter 11

Sally looked at her watch. 7:28 pm. She finished the last notes in her case file and started to pack her things into her briefcase.

She had no intentions of being any later than she was already.

Billington rubbed her hands under the air drier; she hated the things, so noisy. She pulled the handle of the bathroom door towards her just as Sally walked in, almost bumping into each other, and apologising at the same time.

"This is awkward," Sally thought to herself. They both stood in front of each other; without saying a word, Billington made the first move. She moved towards Sally, whose heart was about to rip through her blouse. Without hesitation, the woman pressed herself against Sally, and their lips met. Billington put her hands on Sally's shoulders and pinned her against the toilet door, hoping the cleaners had left the building. Sally's thoughts turned to Steve; she needed to tell him she was going to be late. Possibly very late.

Chapter 12

Steve fell asleep close to midnight. He didn't hear the news on TV about a private jet crashing off the coast of France. He didn't hear the front door, the shower, or even Sally climb into bed. He certainly didn't hear her say she loved him.

Chapter 13

Three days passed, and Sally was getting anxious. She had heard nothing from her father.

That evening, she drove to his house. As she drove up the drive, she began to feel sick. A few moments later, she slammed on the brakes, and the car skidded on the gravel. She opened the door of the car and threw up on the ground. She could hear her father's voice in her head, shouting at her for making skid marks. Sadly, the voices were only in her imagination.

She convinced herself that she had eaten something that didn't agree with her. The spare key to the porch was still under the pottery snail where it had always been.

The front door opened into the vast, modern hallway, but she hated the house. It was made of concrete squares. The floors were also concrete but highly polished and cool to the touch, but, somehow, the house was always warm.

The house possessed state of the art glass panels that could turn black at the push of a button allowing complete privacy.

She smiled as she recalled a summer when her parents were away on one of their many cruising holidays, and she spent the day naked in the house. She had deliberately left the panels transparent as the postman arrived and she sat on the stairs pretending to be both making a phone call and oblivious to his arrival. She loved the fact that the poor chap had probably gone back to the depot and told all his colleagues what had happened. There were many wrong deliveries that week.

The house looked different. She walked around and, eventually, walked into the master bedroom. There was a walk-in wardrobe, and all her father's clothes were still there.

She returned to sit on the stairs in the exact spot as when she made her fake phone call, picked up the house phone, and dialled the number to his new mobile phone for what felt like the millionth time. Nothing. She spotted a flashing light. There were twelve missed calls and no voice messages, just the sound of deep breathing.

Sally considered calling the police, but, for whatever reason, she didn't.

One day turned into two and time rolled on. Eventually, she decided it was time to report his disappearance.

There had been no news of Robert for weeks. The police, Interpol, and the FBI had pictures but nothing, not a single lead.

Sally was beginning to accept that her father was involved with some extremely undesirable people and that that may have something to do with his disappearance.

All of Robert's assets were in limbo; he had also been halfway through selling a very desirable 1968 Mustang Fastback, a replica from the Bullitt film. Steve wanted this car more than anything, but so did the buyer who had already transferred a £40,000 deposit.

That night, she cried herself to sleep, "Please come home, Dad. Please."

Things were tough; the banks seized everything Robert owned.

The cars, bikes, the house, and an apartment in St Lucia, of which Sally knew nothing. Neither of them knew how much was involved, but one of her fellow solicitors did some digging.

Two figures came up in the enquiries; the bank was owed between one and four million pounds.

Things became quite normal for a while; Sally had been made a partner at work, and Steve turned up every day and got his hands dirty.

All the wedding plans were put on hold, nothing was said about the money that had been paid to the venue. They were concerned the bank may ask for it.

The night summer heat became uncomfortable. Steve decided to give Sally a little more air and made up the spare bed.

Unable to sleep, Sally lay wide-awake.

She looked at the clock again. Just six minuteshad passed since she last checked.

Steve had become quite vocal in bed; she sometimes could make out what he was saying in his dreams but not enough to make any sense.

That night would be different. Very different.

"Nooooo! Nooooooo! Dean! No! No! No . . ."

Sally heard every word clearly. She slipped out of the bed. As quietly as she could, she crept into the spare bedroom. Steve was sitting up. This time, he had not sweated. He looked calm but had a really worried expression on his face. Sally initially felt relieved. As she got closer, she could see Steve was not awake and looked as if he was in a trance or had been hypnotised. Unsure of what to do, Sally slowly sat next to him but kept her distance just in case he flung his arms around.

27

"Dean, Dean." He kept repeating that name and then started a conversation; she assumed it was Dean.

Lots of murmuring followed until, eventually, he became quiet and calm. A few minutes later, Steve lifted the duvet, slid his legs in, and lay down. Seconds later, he was fast asleep. He always breathed in a certain way when he was in a deep sleep; Sally recognised this and slowly got off the bed and returned to her own room where she sat in bed watching the clock, wishing she could get some sleep herself.

Sally's eyes opened, she looked at the clock: 9:09. "Thank God," she thought. She had got some rest. She then remembered what had happened a few hours ago.

She called out, and there was no answer. As she sat up a little more, she saw the note on the pillow next to her:

Gone to work, slept like a log last night and didn't want to wake you, call me if you need me, love U XXXX

Steve felt like shit; he was so worried. It was 7:30 am, and, as usual, he was the first one into work. All he could think about was the dream; he needed to talk to Dean, to warn him.

The routine of opening the business helped pass a little time, but then he sat in the little office next to the workshop, still trying to make sense of things. The back door to the building was right next to the office, and Steve looked up every time the door opened. Each member of the staff would walk through this door; at least, he hoped they would.

Dean always walked into the building at 9:01 am; it was a standing joke between his colleagues about how someone could be a minute late, every day.

8:57, 8:58, 8:59, 9:00 . . .

Steve opened the door at 9:01. No Dean.

His heart was beating so fast, his lips dry. He ached as if he had the flu, and even his knees felt weak.

Keith was the Dealer Principal of the business. Steve made his way to his office. Out of courtesy, he knocked on the door, but, instead of waiting to be invited, he entered.

"Bugger me, you ok mate?" Keith asked.

"I might be getting a cold," Steve said with the quickest response he could think of.

"Is Dean in today?" Steve asked.

"No," was the immediate reply from his boss,

"He is taking his mother to go and see a care home this morning; he will be in later. Do you need something urgently?"

Steve made up an excuse about a part not being left out as it should have been; he apologised to Keith for bothering him and said he will go and look on Dean's desk again.

"This is not good," Steve thought, but he had no idea what he should do.

How the hell can you phone a chap you work with and say:

"Hi Dean, its Steve at work, be careful today will you because I think it's your day to die."

The morning dragged and every minute seemed like an hour.

It was so difficult to concentrate on what he was supposed to be doing, but, in between looking at his watch and the big station clock on the workshop wall, Steve finally finished the work on the car he started four hours ago.

He walked up the dirty, steel staircase to what was fondly known as the mess room. It was a room above the workshop containing a table, chairs, a microwave that had so much bacteria and charred remains only the hardest of men even opened the door, a sink full of dirty cups, and a kettle, which took so long to boil, some of the guys walked down to the vending machine, because it was quicker.

The best thing in this room was the cool wall. Based on a well-known TV motoring programme, this cool wall didn't contain pictures of cars; it was covered in pictures ripped out of pornographic magazines. Occasionally, if a female member of staff was going to use the mess room, one of the technicians who would run ahead and turn the board around, hopefully in good time. Occasionally, this happened a little too late, causing embarrassment for some.

The pictures changed daily.

Steve sat there with three of his fellow technicians. He looked at his watch; it was 1:30 pm.

A minute later Dean walked through the door. Steve jumped out of his seat, walked over to Dean, put his arms around him, and hugged him.

Dean was shocked. "What's up, bud?" he said.

Rather embarrassed, Steve pretended it was all a bit of a joke, saying it was unusual for him to have time off, and he was missed.

Steve felt dizzy. He patted Dean on the back, walked down the stairs and onto the valet wash bay, stood over the drain, and threw up. Five minutes later, he was back at his hoist and looking at a leaking sump.

Sally had dinner on the table waiting for Steve to get in. She had been trying to figure out what to say to him all day, but when he walked in, she was so pleased to see him, all she could do was put her arms around him and hold him. She began to cry.

They sat at the dining table, Steve had a homemade lasagne with garlic bread and Sally had a smoothie.

"We need to talk," she said. "What's going on Steve? Your nightmares are frightening me; I never know what to do."

Sally told Steve about the nightmare the previous night. She was worried, a genuine concern. She loved him with every molecule of existence she said.

Steve was thinking quickly about how much he should tell Sally, not wanting to upset her, but at the same time, he didn't want her to think he was going mad.

They both agreed to sit down after dinner and talk about it. Steve had a while longer to decide what to say.

Chapter 14

When is a lie acceptable? We all do it.

Is it ok to hide something to protect someone?

If we all told the truth all the time, the world would fall apart.

Politicians can't tell the truth, if they did no one would believe them.

The fabric of our daily lives is peppered with lies from the moment we are born.

It's best we don't think about it too much, otherwise we will doubt everything everyone says to us.

Protecting those we love with the non-truth is sometimes called being economical with the truth. This is still a lie.

Telling the truth can hurt more than being economical with it.

Chapter 15

Sally was on the sofa and Steve in his armchair. There was a glass of San Miguel beer on the coffee table, and Sally was drinking a gin and tonic.

Steve had decided to tell the truth, or he was going to try.

"Tell me about last night," Sally said.

Steve asked for her to listen, to not say a word until he had finished.

"I had a dream; I don't know if it's a nightmare. I can't tell the difference between them at the moment, but I have no idea why this is happening to me. I love you with all my heart and nothing will ever change that, but these dreams I'm having scare me."

Steve took a few gulps of his beer before continuing; he was grateful that Sally hadn't interrupted. He had tears in his eyes and his chest felt tight.

"Last night was different; I remember what happened, and it felt so real. It was like I was having an out of body experience.

I remember standing in a room; I can't describe the room, because there was nothing in it except a white table.

In front of me was a book. I don't know how big the book was.

It was a white book, an open book, and I could see names." Steve paused for another few mouthfuls of his drink. Sally was still sitting quietly.

"Not just names; there were three columns on the page, the page was full of names in the first column, then the second column was dates, the third was . . ."

Steve stopped talking, reached for his glass, and drained it. He held it in his hands as tears rolled down his cheeks. He took a breath.

"The third column was how they are going to die."

Steve stood up, visibly shaking. He went to the kitchen, opened the fridge, and returned with a cold bottle of water.

He sat back in the chair and began to drink the water from the bottle.

They both sat in silence for a while. It was Sally who spoke first.

"Was it Dean's name you saw in the book last night?" she asked him.

"How the hell did you know that?"

Steve stood up, genuinely surprised Sally knew.

The two of them sat in front of each other, and Sally described how she found Steve sitting on the bed in a trance, that the name she heard him repeat was Dean's. Steve looked down at the floor. He told her when he arrived at work, Dean wasn't in and his relief when, after lunch, the man turned up.

Sally looked at the man in front of her.

This is the man who was her world, her rock, her stability in life, but, in this moment, she barely recognised him.

"Sweetheart, it was a dream, or a nightmare; we all dream, it's not real. Who knows why we think these things."

Steve sat quietly; he could hear words coming from Sally's mouth, but he wasn't listening. He was thinking about the dream; he could see Dean's name.

He knew what was going to happen, but there was one thing that bothered him; as much as he could see the book in his mind, there was one thing he could not see: the date.

The two of them sat in silence. Sally wanted to say something that would make him feel better, but she struggled to find the words.

They lay in bed, holding each other. Both were frightened to fall asleep; it took a while, but soon, they were breathing heavily.

Sally had begun to work more from home and often spent whole days visiting clients. One of her colleagues, the pretty red head who always wore a suit, would often accompany her.

Steve knew Sally liked her, and she seemed happy when the woman arrived at the house early to pick her up for client visits. Besides, Steve also secretly liked the way the woman dressed; her skirts were short, and he often caught a glimpse of her stocking tops. He decided not to say anything that might upset Sally.

Sally's parent's house was repossessed by the bank, along with everything in it. Steve was obviously gutted about the contents of the garage. One evening, he went over to the house. He knew where the spare key was for the garage. He got in and filled his car with tools. This weren't just any tools but a huge collection of Snap On tools and worth a fortune. He didn't tell anyone and had to hide them in his own garage for a while.

Nothing was heard from Robert. Steve had his suspicions, but he kept those to himself.

Life began to settle down again, and everyone seemed content.

Sally joined a gym in the town; she was always conscious of her body and loved to keep trim. He was very proud of her. She was looking better than ever, and, along with her improved fitness, her sexual appetite increased. That was something Steve was very happy about.

Chapter 16

Steve woke up with a jump. He was drenched in sweat. He didn't call out but sat in bed. He was breathing heavily and as quietly as he could he got out of bed. Sally was snoring loudly, so he crept out of the bedroom and walked into the bathroom.

Sitting on the side of the bath, he closed his eyes. He could see the columns, clear as day.

Column 1: Alan Jacobs

Column 2: 28th September

Column 3: Water

So much was going through his mind; what the hell was happening to him? Water? Drowning?

What is this? Why me? He quietly sat in the bathroom and tried to calm himself down.

There was no way he could return to bed; he crept downstairs and into the kitchen to get a drink. Sitting in the lounge in his pants, he thought about what he had seen. He hadn't even given Alan a second thought since Sandra's party. He picked up and looked through the local phone directories to find Alan's company number. He couldn't miss it; a whole page was dedicated to ACJ Logistics in Southampton.

Steve ripped the page out, folded it, and put it in his lunchbox with the sandwiches Sally made for his lunch. He saw the Kit Kat wafer and, for a moment, contemplated eating it. He closed the fridge, opened the cupboard, and took a Kit Kat from what Sally called the naughty box.

His diet was a constant irritation to Sally; she was determined to introduce him to proper food, eventually.

Picking the phone up as soon as he got to work, he opened his lunchbox, took the page from the directory, and phoned the number.

To his surprise, the phone was answered almost immediately.

"ACJ, how can I help"? a very bubbly voice said.

"Is Alan in today, please?" asked Steve.

The reply left him lost for words.

"The little sod is in Guernsey and won't be back until October the 11th. He got a new boat. Can you believe it? Alan, on a boat. The silly bugger can't even swim," she laughed.

He hung up. He walked into the mess room and looked at the calendar on the wall. Today's date was the 29th.

It was a long day, and Steve couldn't wait to get home. He had to tell Sally about Alan.

It was the wettest day of the year, and it took Steve twice as long to get home. The walk from his car to the house was only a few meters. Far enough to drench him. Once inside, he stood on the doormat. Sally sat in the lounge, watching TV. He looked at his beautiful partner and had a sudden head rush. He felt dizzy for a second. He trudged over and kissed Sally. His heart was pounding in his chest, as he looked at her.

He made a split-second decision not to tell Sally about Alan. "It's just a dream," he thought to himself. "Just another dream . . .

I need food," he announced looking at her.

"I need you," was the reply.

An hour later, the two of them ended up driving to the local fish and chip shop.

Chapter 17

OCTOBER 11th

Steve was the first one in at work as usual.

The clock display showed 7:31am, he picked the phone up and rang the number.

It was answered straight away.

"ACJ" It was a man's voice, Steve was disappointed, he liked the girl he spoke to last time.

"Can I talk to Alan please?"

There was a long pause.

"Can I ask who is calling please?" came the reply.

Steve said he was an old friend of Alan's, and he wanted to know if he could help with moving some furniture. At that split second, he thought about how stupid that sounded. He need not have worried.

"My name is Detective Sergeant Paul Boyce from Hampshire Constabulary. Would it be possible for you to come to Southampton Police Station Mr . . . ?"

Steve hung up.

Ten seconds later, the phone rang; it was the detective.

"Sorry about that; we got cut off," he said.

Steve apologised; he agreed to go to the police station at lunchtime. He didn't want Sally to know anything about it and decided not to say a word to the police about his dream.

The meeting at the police station took ten minutes; the on-duty policeman took a statement to confirm the relationship.

The officer was quite happy to tell Steve that Alan had gone missing.

Apparently, they found his new boat adrift only two miles outside St. Peter Port. There was no sign of life on the brand- new motorboat (worth in excess of £200k).

The only other thing the officer knew was that Alan had set off at 5 am from St. Peter Port on the 28th, and they thought he may have fallen overboard. Guernsey RNLI and harbour police had done quite an extensive search of the area with no results to date.

Steve asked the young PC to keep him informed if there were any changes, knowing full well he was unlikely to hear anything.

Steve felt uncomfortable and quite sick. Why was he having these dreams, visions, or whatever it was?

What should he do?

Who should he talk to?

The rest of the day was blurry with one exception; Sally called and asked if he minded her going out that evening with the girls in the office.

Taking it as an opportunity to have a couple of beers and watch a film, he agreed.

Chapter 18

Steve felt Sally getting into bed beside him. He pretended to be asleep but managed to glance at the clock (3:15 am), wondering where she had been all night. It was no time to be having a conversation, and the last 24 hours had made him mentally exhausted. He lay there for another fifty minutes before falling asleep.

At 5:50 am, the alarm went off, it was routine to wait for the nine-minute snooze alarm to go off before getting out of bed. This morning was quite different.

Without saying a word, Sally disappeared underneath the quilt, gently running her tongue around his manhood.

He still got out of bed on time, feeling very relieved and grateful that his beautiful little lady enjoyed having sex with him.

Sally lay in bed and, while listening to the shower, she licked her fingers and slid them between her legs. It didn't take her long to orgasm; she bit her lip to stop moaning out loud, but if anyone could have seen her face it was obvious what she had been doing.

By the time Steve returned to the bedroom, Sally pretended to be asleep. Life seemed to return to normality for a while.

Steve continued his daily routine, and Sally was enjoying being more involved in the firm, where longer hours were expected.

It was easier to accept because partner life was good. There was still talk of a wedding, and, because the cost had been paid by Sally's missing father, they decided on a date. Two days later, their plans were blown apart. The TV news report announced,

"It is with great sadness that Royston Castle in Dorset has to close due to unforeseen circumstances; all deposits and monies paid will be returned and we sincerely apologise for any inconvenience."

That evening, it was discovered that Robert had paid £100k for the wedding.

The money was refunded into Steve's bank account the following day with mixed emotions; they both felt sad because it was a gift from Robert, but, on the other hand, £100k was a lot of money and would prove to be very helpful.

The money was used to open a new account, in Steve's name; they called it the rainy-day money.

It was a lot more helpful than either of them could imagine but not necessarily for the right reason.

Steve's dreams had stopped, or so he thought.

He felt guilty at times, there's no way he could have done anything to help Sally's parents, but could he have warned Alan?

These thoughts haunted Steve. He had now crossed the line in being able to talk to Sally, or anyone, about what had happened.

Even if he and Alan had met, how do you approach the conversation?

"Hi Alan, I know we haven't spoken for a long while but don't go near any water because you are going to die.

This is the makings of a crackpot," he thought.

Chapter 19

Sandra sat at the end of her bed, stroking her beloved British Blue cat who she had named after her father. It was a strange thing to do, but it was his money that bought her everything.

She was grateful he had come into her life, but she was still very bitter about the years her mother had brought her up alone. For many years as she was growing up, she referred to her father as "Non- Dad".

It was when she was in her early teens that she started asking questions about why he wasn't around, and her mother, Claire, had always said that they just didn't love each other enough to stay together.

It was a few years later that the two of them sat down and talked.

Sandra remembered that day as if it were yesterday. One morning, as she was leaving for school, her mother told her she wanted to talk to her about something that evening. Sandra was just over sixteen and had assumed that the chat would have been about the rumour going around the school about her being caught fingering one of her classmates in the bathroom cubicle. Sandra had regretted being caught—not regretted the incident—just being caught.

On returning home from school, her mother was sitting in the lounge at the dining table. There was also a suitcase on the table. The contents of the case were going to provide answers, but they were also going to shape Sandra's life, unfortunately, not necessarily for the best.

Sandra could see tears in her mother's eyes as she apologised for not being completely honest with her.

Claire told Sandra what she thought her daughter needed to know; the full truth was to be kept a secret for a while longer.

Claire had become pregnant because of a one-night stand; she had gone to a party with her friends and met a group of boys from the local technical college. One of the boys, who was from a very "posh" family, had taken a liking to Claire. They snuck off together into the large garden.

The boy had put his jacket on the ground near the large pond, and they laid watching the stars together.

Sandra's mother spared her of the exact details, but nine months later, she was born.

Claire was just eighteen, and her parents had tried to get her to have her baby adopted. She insisted on keeping her little girl.

"What was his name?" Sandra remembered asking her mother repeatedly.

Claire eventually opened the case, took an envelope out, and opened it; she gave the picture to her daughter.

With tears rolling down her face, Sandra looked at the picture.

A very handsome lad sat on a motorbike, his hair all swept back. He was dressed in a nice pair of grey trousers, wearing a college tie, white shirt, and a matching jacket. He looked very smart.

On the back of the picture was written,

"Forever in my heart, all the world and a sixpence xx Robert X."

Both women sat there crying, looking at the picture.

There were many letters in the case; Claire picked one out and gave it to Sandra. She read it.

She learned that her father could not be a part of her life, because it would affect his studies. He was due to go to college and was too young to have children.

The two of them talked and sat together, occasionally holding each other and crying. It was 5 am when they went to bed.

Two years later, things changed.

It was Sandra's 18th, and she had a birthday card and letter that literally changed her world. The letter read:

Sandra,

This is the hardest thing I have ever written. If I could have changed things years ago, I would have.

We have never met, and it's the biggest regret of my life.

Just over eighteen years ago, I met the most wonderful loving young lady, the same woman you call mother.

Unfortunately, our lives were totally different; our parents were not as supportive as they should have been of our relationship.

There are few words I can use that will ever make up for eighteen years of your life I have missed. I regret that I will never be able to be the father you deserve.

I know your mother has struggled to do the best for you, so I have decided to send you some money.

I would prefer you kept this from your mother, as I would assume she would not want me to do this.

If you want to think of it as guilt payment, I understand.

You may do with it as you please. You will never hear from me again, and I wish with all my heart that you will be happy in whatever road your life takes you.

You are in my thoughts every day.

Rx

Inside the card was a cheque for two hundred and fifty thousand pounds.

The letter had a huge impact on Sandra; it took her just over five months to pay the cheque into her bank account, and she didn't use a penny for another six.

It took a lot of soul searching to begin with, but, in the end, it was two things that made her revalue her life. The "One Life Live It" motto was the first thing, at the same time she also became friendly with a young man who was admitted into the hospital where she was training, he had been involved in a horrific car accident. Unfortunately, his injuries were so severe he would have never been able to have any kind of life, he knew he only had a few days to live but was one of the most funny, humble and sincere people you could have ever met, he died looking into her eyes and holding her hand.

Sandra never told her mother about the money; it did make her feel guilty to begin with but as time went on, she just accepted it was her ticket to a better life.

The one thing she did ask her mother was if she had ever heard from Robert.

She suspected the two of them made contact because Claire never really answered her questions, she used to cleverly avoid the subject stating it was the present and future which are important and not the past.

Sandra also wondered why her mother had never asked her about her finances, there was one possible reason for this, she wondered if her mother knew more than she let on.

Chapter 20

A dream is a dream, right?

That felt so real, thank god it was only a dream.

Or was it?

What happens when your sleep dreams come true?

Surely that depends on if it was a nice dream. What If, just what If, it's the nasty dream that comes true?

Will you be afraid to go to sleep in case things get worse?

Get worse!

How the hell can they get worse than seeing someone you know is going to die?

Chapter 21

Steve typed in:

How can we induce dreams?

How can we remember dreams?

How can I get back to a dream?

Steve was up late watching TV. Sally was not due home until 10 at the earliest; it was 11:05 as he keyed the questions into the laptop.

Nothing came up to satisfy his curiosity; there were lots of reasons why we dream, even some interesting interpretations of dreams but not the answers Steve wanted.

Getting into bed at 1 am with still no Sally, he fell asleep straight away.

Chapter 22

Sally gently opened the front door. She looked around at the new silver Audi TT; she waved and watched Billington drive slowly away. Her heart sank for a moment before closing the door as silently as possible.

She crept into the kitchen and, finding a bottle of water on the worktop, she opened it and drank its contents.

Again, being as quiet as possible, she walked into the lounge. "Just five minutes on the sofa," she thought to herself; a few seconds later, she was fast asleep.

Steve woke her by kissing her forehead. She was still on the sofa, and it was just after 6 am.

He asked her nicely to try not to stay at work so late; he didn't want to lecture her but was concerned for her wellbeing.

Sally wasn't listening. She wanted to go up to bed, but she was also conscious of her panties sticking out of her handbag. She was hoping Steve wouldn't notice. He didn't.

Things became settled again. There was still no sign of Robert and, as time went on, Sally just accepted that he may have come to a sticky end. She never let Steve know she suspected something bad had happened; she just dealt with it.

Sally had made much more of an effort to work sensible hours and that enabled her to spend more time with Steve.

To his relief, his dreams seemed to have subsided. He would still dream but often woke laughing because the dream had been so silly or had nothing to do with the nightmares he had previously.

Every day he got to work, he was relieved to see Dean.

It had been a while since the dream about him and, thankfully, the man was alive and well. The two colleagues had become more friendly towards each other now, and Steve was now aware that Dean's mother was in a care home not too far away from where they lived. Dean had also told Steve he had been doing some online dating. His 11-year affair had finally decided to stay with her husband.

The two of them looked at a brochure from a dating website he had been sent.

"Russian brides for professionals."

Steve looked through the pages and wondered if the pictures were genuine. From what he had seen, it made interesting reading. Dean had already made the £500 down payment to go to Russia and meet one of the ladies. She wasn't in the brochure, but he was waiting for a photo to be sent to him.

Steve had his suspicions but decided to keep things to himself as Dean sounded and looked excited.

Steve couldn't forget that Dean had featured in one of his dreams. "Just a matter of time," he thought. "It's only a matter of time until we all die, including me."

Sally called Steve at work; after moaning again about him not having a mobile phone, she said they needed to talk that evening, and she would cook a nice meal. She ended the call with the words,

"Don't worry it's all good news."

It was certainly rare for the two of them to sit down together. There was a bottle of red wine and a pint of Steve's favourite beer in a cold glass. The lamb shank and roasted vegetables were sitting in front of them.

Sally went on to tell Steve all about the changes at work, how well the business was doing but also the planned expansion and that the company had taken over another company in the New Forest, dealing with all legal matters in the marine industry.

Sally then told Steve the partners want her to take over the new business. She and one other member of the team have been offered the chance to expand their Lymington office.

Steve sat in silence. He listened to every word, and, the more he looked at Sally, he could see in her eyes how excited she was.

She continued, ". . . look at this."

She placed a brochure for a beautiful Cob Cottage in front of him, complete with nearly an acre of land. The picture was of a white house with perfectly manicured lawns and a large purpose built wooden building that would be an ideal office and dark room. It looked amazing.

Steve looked at her again.

"Hun," she said as she leaned over the table.

She took Steve's hand.

"Hun, you could give up work if you wanted. Start your own business. I honestly don't mind, please think about it."

Steve looked at her, smiled and said,

"Ok. Let's do it."

She stood up, almost knocking the dinner table to the floor. Throwing her arms around him, she kissed him, holding him tighter than ever, and she began to cry.

They looked at each other, tears rolling down Sally's face. Steve could see what this had meant to her.

She grabbed Steve's hand again. He sat on the sofa next to her and told him that in the morning they were going to see the house and look around. She also told him that she had already phoned his work and got him the day off.

Steve never did find out how she did that.

Two months later, they moved into the cottage.

Sally worked at home in the beautiful, detached, purpose-built office. When he could, Steve worked on the house and in the garden. There certainly seemed enough to do, and the thought of giving up work seemed worth considering.

Two months into their new life, Sally was sitting at her desk when her phone rang.

She watched Steve cutting the grass as she sat in the office. The fresh smell that only grass can produce filled the air. The sun was high, and it felt like a perfect summer's day.

Steve peered into the office as he walked past with the lawn mower. His beloved partner was on the phone. She looked deep in thought. He blew her a kiss, and she blew one back.

Luckily, Steve couldn't hear what was being said on the phone. Sally sat quietly listening. Without saying a word, she hung up; her stomach was churning.

"You bitch," she said. "You little bitch."

He had no idea how life could change so quickly, but he was going to find out, soon.

It was late when they both got into bed, Steve fell asleep straight away; the clean air and lack of stress helped him sleep. Sally lay wide- awake, going over the phone call she received that afternoon.

Chapter 23

Steve was in the room, white, everything white, blank walls, no windows, alone. It didn't even feel as if he is in the room; he couldn't see his arms, body, or legs, but he was looking around slowly.

There was a white table, a simple white oblong table with white legs. On the table was a book.

The book was open. There are so many pages, he couldn't count them. The pages were blank. There was no feeling of a draught, but the pages began to move, going from right to left as if someone were turning them. Still, they were all blank. Just white pages, no sound, nothing.

Very slowly, the pages slowed down, eventually stopping on two blank sheets in front of him.

Lines appeared in front of him, two lines in black on the left page, going from the top of the page to the bottom. Steve now looked as hard as possible for the columns to be filled with something legible, something he could make sense of.

"It's coming." The writing slowly began. In block capitals, the letter "S" appears.

There was no air in the room at all. All Steve could see was the page in front of him. Suddenly, the page turned. As much as he tried, he couldn't turn the page back.

In front of him, as clear as it could be, was written:

Column 1: His name

Column 2: 22nd of March

Column 3: Shot

Steve sat up in bed. He felt calm, but it took a moment to realise he was alone. It took even longer to realise what he had just seen in his dream.

He felt so calm, unexpected for a man who had just seen the day and manner of his own death. It was still early, and his alarm had not gone off. He got out of bed and went over to the window. Looking into the garden, he could see the office door open.

Sitting back down on the bed, he was disorientated. "What do I tell Sally?" he thought.

Standing up again, he put his shorts on. It was a beautiful morning. The sun had yet to fill the garden, and, looking out of the window again, he could hear Sally's voice coming from the office.

He walked down the tiny narrow staircase and went into the bathroom for a pee and washed his hands and face with the lovely smelling Moulton Brown soap.

He walked through the lounge and into the kitchen. The back door was wide open. The office was only a few meters from the kitchen.

Sally stood up quickly when she saw Steve. She had been sitting on the old chesterfield sofa that was seeing its last days out in the office. She was wearing her white cotton dressing gown, and she looked flushed.

Standing behind the sofa was Billington, looking very sweaty. She was wearing her bright orange lycra jogging outfit, and Steve couldn't help notice her huge breasts. He had met her a number of times and was surprised to see her.

Billington's swanky cliff top apartment was only three miles away. He suspected his beautiful partner was having more than a good working relationship with the woman. Secretly, he wouldn't blame her for doing so.

Steve said hi, apologised for interrupting them, and offered to make both women something to drink, which they kindly declined. He excused himself and went into the kitchen to make some breakfast. Sally turned around to see Billington pulling up her jogging trousers.

They both had to muffle their giggles.

"Fuck, that was close," Sally said with a huge smile.

In that moment, Steve decided not to tell Sally about the dream.

Steve decided his life *had* to change.

Chapter 24

Steve's head was pounding; he was trying to make sense of everything. He sat at the dining table, holding the cup of tea in his hands. The cup was so hot, he would have normally put it down to cool off for fifteen minutes. Today, he held the cup. He couldn't feel the heat.

Closing his eyes, he could see the page in front of him as if he had taken a photograph.

Definitely his name, the date (a few months away), shot? Who would want to shoot him and why? Steve was trying to build a puzzle with no clues or instructions; it didn't make sense.

Going through the list in his head, he remembered Sally's mother, Patricia; "She was going to die at some point," he thought, but he had woken at the exact time, hadn't he?

Robert was still missing and nothing had been heard from him. He was in deep debt, but the debtor remained unknown.

Alan was also still missing. Had he drowned like everyone had suspected?

Dean! He was perfectly well. Alive and kicking and more than likely beginning to enjoy life. Now his dream, his name.

What should he do?

Sally walked into the lounge, walked over to Steve, and wrapped her arms around his shoulders. She lowered her head and kissed his cheek. This brought Steve back to reality; he turned his head and their lips met.

He stood up and turned towards the beautiful figure in front of him. Sally opened her dressing gown to reveal her stunning figure. He moved closer, put his hands under her bottom and lifted her on to the dining table. She leaned back supporting herself on her arms, Steve lowered his head and kissed Sally's neck. His kisses were getting lower.

Steve still left home for work at the usual time. He opened up the business, then sat in the mess room looking at the new pictures on the cool wall while waiting for his tea to cool down.

He realised some of the pictures were new and smiled to himself. One picture caught his eye; he walked over to the picture and stared at it closer.

There was no doubt in his mind that the face he was looking at was familiar. The red headed woman was sitting on a chesterfield sofa that looked exactly like the one in Sally's office. More precisely, it was without doubt their sofa. The girl he recognised was not alone; between her legs, on all fours, was another girl with shoulder length blonde hair and a tattoo of a black cat on her left shoulder. Both women were naked.

Steve removed the picture and put it in his trouser pocket then sat back down just as one of his fellow technicians walked into the room.

Every time Steve was alone that morning, he took the picture out and looked at it. "At least it's taken my mind off that dream," he thought to himself.

At lunchtime, he walked into the dealer principal's office and told his boss Keith that he had completely forgotten he had a dental appointment and pleaded with the man to let him have the afternoon off. His boss reluctantly agreed to let him go.

Chapter 25

Steve sat in his car; he felt guilty about lying.

Less than an hour later, he was in the car park overlooking the sea. Boscombe Beach below him was packed. It was a lovely day. He could see people were enjoying their day. A few brave souls were swimming, others were enjoying the last few days of sun before the bad weather set in.

He closed his eyes; and it took seconds for him to fall asleep.

Chapter 26

There was a tapping on the window of the car. It took a few moments for Steve to focus. It was also getting dark.

She stood by the car, looking at the man inside. She thought to herself he looked kind, but, at the same time, she could see there was something troubling him.

The window went down.

"Hello, are you ok?" she asked.

Steve looked at the girl; she was probably in her mid-twenties, had bronze skin, brown short hair in a bob style, dark eyes, and a thin face. He recognized her accent was Greek. She was very athletic, wearing a half cropped white sports top and lycra trousers. They enhanced her figure and left little to the imagination.

She leaned further into the car and Steve could smell her perfume. He recognised the smell as his favourite, the unmistakable smell of Escape by Calvin Klein.

What possessed him to reply, he would never know, but, in less than a minute, she was sitting next to him.

Chapter 27

Mari wasn't afraid to sit with her new friend and tell him her life's story. As a nurse in her native Greek island of Corfu, she loved her work but was always keen to travel. The wages in Corfu were not as good as those in the UK, so she had been applying for a number of positions. So far, she hadn't received a response from any of them.

One evening, she was out with a friend in Corfu Town, and they had met a group of girls on holiday from Bournemouth in the South of England, one of them was a nurse and they became very good friends. It was this friend who managed to get Mari a placement at Bournemouth Hospital.

That was two years ago, and she had fallen in love with living in Dorset and had made a new life, the only thing missing was a good man, someone she could look after and love.

Steve looked at his watch: 8:15.

Blind panic set in, and he had a moment of clarity. Apologising profusely, he told Mari he had to go home. She found an old petrol receipt on the floor of the car and wrote her number on it with an IKEA pencil.

Driving far too fast, Steve headed for home, his mind totally in a whirl now. What was he going to tell Sally when he got in? He thought about Mari. He assumed she wanted to be more than just friends, but he could have misunderstood her. Maybe she was just a good Samaritan.

Steve pulled up to the drive and noticed Sally's car was not there. The house was in complete darkness. He walked down the pitch- black path to the back door. Unlocking the door, he switched the kitchen light on.

On the wipe clean board on the kitchen wall, he read:

"Sorry Hun, B home at 10, LUV U XXXX."

Steve switched all the lights on downstairs, put the TV on, and changed into his tatty jogging bottoms and T-shirt before crashing out on the sofa.

He lay there, his heart still pounding from rushing around. He was happy to see an old episode of Top Gear on the television and, within minutes, was laughing aloud.

Two minutes later, Sally walked in. She apologised for not being there when he got home.

"How was your day?" she asked.

"Same old, same old," Steve replied.

Sally rolled her eyes at him and went upstairs to change. Steve lay on the sofa.

"More lies," he thought to himself. "More lies."

He went up to bed first, and it didn't take him long to fall asleep.

Sally sat on the sofa, listening to make sure he was asleep; she gave him another fifteen minutes and then opened the back door. Moments later, she sat in her office and was on the phone. In her other hand, she held a picture ripped out of a porn magazine, a picture she took. Despite everything that had happened earlier, Steve slept for hours until he suddenly woke.

"Shit, shit." He could hear Sally next to him thanks to her tell-tale heavy breathing. He got out of bed as quietly as he could and looked at the alarm clock: 3:27 am.

Creeping as slowly as possible, he went downstairs and into the bathroom. He opened the laundry bin to find his dirty jeans were gone. His heart skipped a beat. He went into the kitchen and opened the now finished washing machine. His jeans still felt slightly warm. As he reached into the right pocket, his heart skipped another beat, and he felt hot and sick.

In a blind panic, he put his hand in the back pocket and found the crumpled piece of paper, all shrivelled up and partially stuck to itself. He tried to open it up but couldn't make out anything resembling the magazine picture.

Putting the clothes back in the washing machine, Steve sat on the kitchen floor. He never put anything in his back pocket, or perhaps he did?

Sally wasn't asleep; she heard the door and even heard the unmistakable sound of the washing machine open. She knew exactly what Steve was looking for and wanted to tell him he would never find the picture. She wanted to know how he got it. She had lots of questions, but she had more secrets than questions. She was still pretending to be asleep when he got back into bed.

Chapter 28

The following morning, all seemed normal in the house.

Steve had convinced himself that the cutting had been completely destroyed.

Sally heard his car reverse off the drive. She got out of bed and pulled her jogging shorts out of the top drawer. She put on her sports bra while admiring her tits and smiled.

In the office minutes later, she reached up on the top shelf and took down a box file. Written on the file was Bournemouth National Health. It had always made her smile. "Thank goodness for the NHS, especially the nurses," she thought.

She sat behind her desk and opened the file; there it was, the picture of Sandra on all fours, her face buried between Billington's legs, who's expression was one of total pleasure, Sally frowned for a second thinking that they should have used more eyeliner on Billington's beautiful eyes. Then the phone rang.

Chapter 29

Steve's lunch was always at 1 pm; he sat with his colleagues, listening to them talk about last tonight's Bournemouth football match, but his mind was elsewhere.

A moment later, Dean walked into the room.

"Steve, there's a customer asking after you outside; she said you look after her."

The other guys in the room all cheered.

Steve walked down the stairs and out into the yard. Standing there in front of him was Mari.

Shocked to see her but also slightly embarrassed, Steve greeted her and led her out of sight to save any questions from his work mates. "What are you doing here? How did you find me? What do you want?"

There were more questions in his head, but he gave her a moment to answer.

Mari said that she wanted to know that he was ok and asked if they could meet for a drink.

She pointed out that finding him was easy as he was in a sign written company car, the address and telephone number in big print along the side of his car. Steve had forgotten about that; he was so used to driving that car that he never gave it any thought.

Mari walked back to her car feeling pleased with herself; she had big plans for Steve and herself.

It was Dean who said something first, asking if Steve had "a bit on the side". Not wanting to draw any attention to the visitor, Steve told Dean that he had looked at her car for her, as she was a friend of the family.

Dean seemed happy with that explanation but winked and smiled at Steve as he walked off.

That afternoon, Steve had lots on his mind. He was thinking about the dream, the picture of Sally's huge breasted colleague, and the other girl on the sofa in Sally's office. He was now wondering what Mari wanted. On top of all this, he was supposed to be servicing three cars. His mind was certainly not on his work. He lowered the ramp of the car he was working on, got in it, and reversed it into the parking space opposite his bay. He handed the keys to the workshop manager.

A routine service should not take too long; there are more checks than actual replacement of items. The most important of items were the oil and filter.

On Steve's workbench sat a new filter for the car he just drove out. The old filter was in his bin. Had he put the new oil in the car, he would have realised that he had just made a big mistake, a mistake that would change the rest of his life.

Chapter 30

That evening, Sally seemed to be very touchy. She hadn't prepared any dinner for them, which was rare, and, rather than starve, she picked up Chinese. The two of them sat in silence as they ate the meal sitting on their laps. The TV was on louder than usual.

Neither Steve nor Sally decided to give in; they hardly spoke at all that evening. Steve assumed Sally had had a bad day and took this opportunity to go over in his mind everything that happened in the last couple of days.

Sally was fuming. A telephone call that afternoon from an unknown female with an accent she couldn't pinpoint.

The girl was threatening to expose her and tell Steve about her sordid lifestyle.

"Why was this bitch doing this?"

Sally tried to think about who and why.

The two of them got into bed together, both completely and emotionally exhausted.

Chapter 31

The alarm went off at the usual time. Steve had no idea that this day would be more different than he could have ever expected.

The cool wall in the mess room had some new additions. Steve was almost paranoid that he would see more pictures of someone he recognised. He had even considered the possibility of walking in and seeing a picture of Sally. He wondered if there were pictures of her, the woman in his life. He loved her so much, but, over time, their honesty with each other had subsided and their secrets had grown bigger.

He thought about the times when they would tell each other everything. He couldn't remember when that stopped; he also couldn't remember when he stopped telling his beautiful lady what he had been feeling and, more importantly, about his dreams.

Steve had known about Sally's lady friends; he had accepted this over time but had chosen to never talk to her about her sexuality. They loved each other, and he was happy with that.

"Steve. Steve!" Keith was raising his voice.

Steve turned around to see his boss standing in the doorway. "My office. Now," he said.

Steve walked into the office and shut the door behind him.

Keith was standing behind his desk and didn't look his usual self.

"What the fuck is going on?" Keith said.

He lit a cigarette, which, in all the years Steve had worked there, he had never seen Keith smoke. He took a big drag and blew the smoke out of his nose.

Steve was trying to think what this was all about, but before he could make sense of anything Keith continued,

"I haven't got a clue what's going on in your life and frankly I don't give a toss. All I care about is running this business. I've worked hard to earn this business a good reputation, and our customers come back to us because they trust us.

Yesterday, one of our regular customers dropped his car off for a service, you know him, Steve. It was Mr. Robson, Mr Paul fucking Robson."

Steve's heart missed a beat. If there was one customer everyone disliked more than anyone else, it was Paul Robson. He was a well-known troublemaker, a self-made multi-millionaire, who made his fortune in buying houses in Bournemouth and dividing them into one-bedroom apartments for students.

He had a bad reputation, and no one ever crossed him. He was a brute of a man who punched first then asked questions.

Steve knew of the man; Sally's father used to be his solicitor. The conversation was not going well, and it was going to get a lot worse.

Steve had drained the oil from Robson's Mercedes. Not just any Mercedes, but an AMG C63, a very expensive and beautiful piece of machinery. Again,

Steve's heart missed a beat; he tried to recall doing the filter and filling the car with oil.

He couldn't, because he then remembered, he hadn't. Twenty minutes later, Steve was sitting in his car; he was suspended from work on the grounds of total negligence. There would be an investigation, but Steve knew that he would be sacked.

The company would have to put a new engine in the Mercedes, which could cost up to £40,000. The cost to the business could be much greater.

Robson had a reputation of bankrupting businesses that crossed him. Steve drove to Boscombe, parked the car close to where he met Mari, and sat there. It had just started to rain, and the beach was nearly empty.

There were a few hardy dog walkers and joggers braving the typical British weather. Steve got out of the car and walked the short distance into the town. The first bar he got to was a swanky wine bar. It had been beautifully decorated using lots of old black and white photos of cars and motorcycles.

Steve thought to himself that if he were ever to design the interior of a bar, he would do it exactly like this.

He sat in the window in an old armchair that could have told a thousand tales while looking out of the window at the rain. He sipped his ice cool San Miguel, then looked across the road and could see a branch of his bank. Next to that was another rival bank.

"How convenient," he thought to himself.

He checked his wallet and found what he was looking for: bankcards and a driving licence. The beer went down well. Walking out of the bar, Steve looked over his shoulder. He wanted some company, and he hoped to see Mari.

That's why he was there; he wanted to know how she could help him and wondered if she knew something he didn't. There was a queue inside the bank; it took a while because there was an old man in front of him with a heavy carrier bag of old coins to be cashed in. In front of him stood a blonde woman; she turned to Steve and smiled at him, and he smiled back at her. A few moments later, she looked over her shoulder again,

"Hi Steve," she said.

He then recognised her; it was Sandra. He had not seen her since her party some years ago. Eventually, he stood in front of the young man behind the glass.

"I want to open an account, please," Steve said.

Minutes later, in the bank next door, Steve again stood in front of the bank assistant.

"Please transfer £90,000 into this bank account, and I would like to draw £10,000 in cash."

Being an unusual request, he had to step into an adjoining office and request the transfer again. A few moments later, he was on the street.

He had ten thousand pounds in used notes in his pockets, and the rest were in the new safe account he had opened.

"Hi . . ." Steve turned to see Sandra behind him. "Do you want to go for a drink?" she said.

Moments later, they were back in the swanky bar. They sat at a table at the back of the room; Steve had another beer, while Sandra had a Mojito.

The two of them sat talking for ages, and the beers kept coming. Unaccustomed to consuming large amounts of alcohol, Steve could feel himself getting drunk. He knew his words were slurring, and he felt tired.

Sandra listened to him tell her he was likely to lose his job.

Sandra was listening to every word, especially when Steve started talking about Sally.

Sandra was, without a doubt, a stunning looking woman. She was in her late thirties and had a fantastic figure. She was very petite, possibly just over 5'2", even with her patent high heels on. She had piercing green eyes, perfectly applied make-up, and shoulder length blonde hair, which had been recently cut and styled, Steve listened to her telling him she was living with her ex-boyfriend who dumped her two weeks after he moved down south from Scotland.

She was working for a private clinic in Bournemouth that specialised in cosmetic surgery and paid her exceptionally well. Steve guessed she was on the rebound, but, right now, he didn't care.

When Sandra got up to visit the toilet, he watched her walking away from him, watching her bottom wiggle. It reminded him of Sally in her keep fit outfit, and, for a second, he wondered if she was ok. But only for a second.

As Sandra walked towards Steve, she smiled at him. She was thinking that tonight would be a good night, a very good night indeed. She decided to push things on a little further to gauge his condition so she settled next to him and moved in for a kiss, just a little kiss to let him know things were good.

It was getting late and there was no way Steve could go home.

He looked at his watch: 11:22.

Then, without any conviction, he said to Sandra, "I need to find somewhere to stay tonight. Can I stay at yours?"

He was shocked at the reply, for a moment. It was a straight "No."

A few moments later, his spirit was lifted when she suggested she help him get a room in one of the many hotels in the area, Steve instantly had a vision in his mind of doing a high five to himself.

He still felt rather smug and just hoped he could sober up enough to remember what he hoped would be a special night. Sandra knew exactly where to take Steve.

She had an agreement with one of the local hotels where, if she wanted, she could hire a suite by the hour. This was costly, but, tonight, there would be no charge.

Chapter 32

Sally had already phoned some of Steve's friends to see if he was with them; she was getting more anxious by the minute. This was so out of character for him; she couldn't even remember him being late home, ever.

She kept going over the previous evening in her mind. "What was it she said to upset him?"

There were so many things going on in her life, she started to suspect she had been neglecting their relationship. "Did her man suspect her of having an affair?"

Eventually, Sally got ready for bed; she didn't want to go upstairs, so she grabbed an old blanket out of the airing cupboard and lay on the sofa. She could talk to Steve when he got home.

She was going to have a long wait.

Chapter 33

Sandra sat at the end of the bed, listening to Steve. He was repeating himself now, and it was getting late. She was also busting to go to the bathroom but wanted Steve to feel she was there to comfort him. Eventually, she had to stop him from talking. She did this by turning towards him, and after putting her finger to his lips, she kissed him, her tongue dancing with his.

For a moment, she thought about where his tongue had been. She stifled a giggle as she suspected that she had used her tongue in places he had. She stood up and walked into the bathroom. Her head was spinning, but she had to keep composed.

She also had to admit to herself that she was feeling exceptionally horny. She lifted her skirt and looked at the wet patch in her panties. That confirmed her suspicion. She smiled and bit her lip in excitement.

It was only about 20 miles from here to his house, his bed, his partner, the woman he still loved so much, but also the woman he didn't know any more.

Although feeling quite ill, Steve picked up the phone and dialled the number for work. He left a garbled message on the answerphone to his employer.

The message was brief:

"Message for Keith Higgins, its Steve. I've decided not to come back to work, send any wages you owe me to Sally. I will drop the car off soon, oh, and it's run out of fuel."

Sandra took her time in the bathroom. She showered using the flexible shower attachment and took extra care not to get her hair wet. She even sat on the toilet for another 10 minutes, going over things in her mind.

Looking in the full-length mirror, she admired her body. She had spent an absolute fortune to look the way she did, and, of course, there was the maintenance as well. There were lotions that had cost thousands of pounds and which she wished she had with her. It was all worth it, every penny. "Vanity comes at a price," she thought.

She could usually charge up to a thousand pounds a night, but this night was totally different.

Things had changed a lot since her monthly allowance had stopped.

This was not how she had planned to spend her life, but the money was so good, and she needed it to pay for her extravagant lifestyle. It did have its perks. Looking in the mirror, she cupped her breasts and wondered to herself if she should go bigger or smaller. "Bigger," she thought. "Bigger is best."

She could see it was all worth it. The look on Steve's face was a picture; she knew she needed to put on a good show, and she hoped she was going to enjoy the next few hours very much.

Any thoughts of Sally and work disappeared in a flash when Steve saw the bathroom door open. The most beautiful woman he had ever seen walked towards him. Her eyes glinted in the low light, and she was wearing what looked like very expensive silk French knickers and a matching bra, which only just covered her perfectly firm breasts. For a moment, he wondered how much they had cost her. Thankfully, he didn't ask.

Chapter 34

Sally awoke with a start. It took her a moment to realise she was still on the sofa. There was a knock at the back door. Instantly thinking Steve had lost his key, she stumbled to the door. Looking through the glass, she could see Billington standing there, jogging gear on. She looked as if she had been in the shower, sweat dripping down her forehead and her face glowing red. She was still panting.

She opened the door, and, although disappointed not to see Steve, she was pleased to see who it was.

On noticing Steve's car was not in the drive and seeing the lounge light on, Billington had taken a chance by knocking on the door.

Sally explained she hadn't heard from Steve or seen him since the previous morning. Billington walked into the kitchen and wrapped her arms around Sally, who was sobbing. Sally was beginning to think something serious had happened. She just wanted to know Steve was ok.

Chapter 35

Debbie had been working for AJC logistics since leaving the Navy two years ago. Ever since Alan had gone missing (assumed drowned in Guernsey), she had been an integral part of the business.

She had started off working in the office, answering the phone and making the tea. Thanks to Alan's generosity, she was able to complete an Open University course on bookkeeping and accounts.

She could now account for every penny AJC had in the bank, what was owed by their clients, and, more importantly, she could see who was being paid and how much.

The police had been very thorough with their investigation into Alan's disappearance, looking into every part of ACJ. They were satisfied with the business's practices and could see a very healthy annual profit.

It was not unusual if a company that was having severe financial difficulties would suddenly have its business owners go missing. However, with over £2m in the bank, financial suicide had been ruled out.

Debbie had been very concerned about one aspect of the business and was very surprised the police had not picked up on it.

In July, Debbie had approached Alan about the wages. She had been asked to look after the payroll since her senior had decided to retire. She had queries about three names on the payroll she didn't recognise; one of them was paid a significant amount every month.

Alan explained that the larger amount was one of the original investors in ACJ and the other two were casual drivers that were also investors. Debbie had no choice but to believe Alan; he had always been straight with her, and she had grown very fond of him. He had no idea of this; if he had, things may have been different.

It wasn't unusual for the phone to be ringing continuously when Debbie got into work at five to seven; today was no exception.

She answered the phone in the same way she always did,

"ACJ, How can I help?"

The phone went dead.

The same thing happened at 7:15, 7:48, and 7:56.

The rest of the day was as busy as it always was; thankfully, the two managers of the business worked hard to make things work. It was in their interest to do so, very much in their interest.

Chapter 36

Steve looked around the hotel room; he thought that £199 was a lot of money for a room of that size. There were no tea or coffee making facilities. Not that it mattered at that moment, because there was an ice bucket on the sideboard with a bottle of champagne in it. The champagne should taste good at £100 a bottle but not as good as the beautiful lady standing in front of him.

Sandra stood for a moment at the end of the bed. She moved her hips slowly from side to side, lifted her right hand up to her face, and slowly slid her middle finger into her mouth. Wetting her finger with her tongue, she slid her hand down her body. Steve could see a trail of saliva from Sandra's chin to her cleavage.

She knew what she was doing. She had previously had men ejaculating in their underwear. Generally, that meant that she could get more sleep. Tonight, she needed her lover to stay awake all night if possible.

She was not due back to the clinic for another two days, plenty of time to rest.

Sandra's right hand slid inside her panties. She always tried to make herself orgasm as soon as she could; she referred to it as a perk of the trade. That way, if her date wasn't up to the job, at least she had been satisfied.

She knew exactly what she was doing. She'd had plenty of practice. Her panties were still damp and an orgasm was now only seconds away. She turned her back on Steve. Bending forwards, she slid her panties off, and, still using the fingers on her right hand, she slid two fingers inside herself as she orgasmed. At that moment, she turned her head to watch the expression on the face of her audience. She then slowly stood up, still looking to make sure she could still see Steve's face.

She stood straight. Still looking over her shoulder, her perfectly tanned bottom facing him, she noticed he wasn't looking at her bottom.

Steve was looking at the tattoo of a black cat on her left shoulder.

Chapter 37

Sandra sat in the back of the taxi.

She was going over things in her mind. What was it she said to him that had triggered that reaction?

Her hand in the panties routine never failed.

Was he really feeling guilty about Sally like he said, or was it something else?

Sandra wondered if Sally ever thought about Steve as she was screwing her latest lover. She doubted it.

Then, for a moment, Sandra wondered if she should pay Sally a visit. She decided it was a bad idea.

It was time to go home to get some sleep. That was when the taxi driver turned round. He looked and smiled at her. She was one of his regulars, and he hoped she would pay the fare like she did last time.

Chapter 38

Going through the last few days in his mind, Steve was trying to make sense of things. What the hell had happened earlier? Was this all really happening to him and why?

A few moments later, his eyes closed. The glass of champagne he was holding lay on the bed, its contents soaking into the covers.

Chapter 39

Sally sat in her office, still wearing yesterday's clothes. The phone was in her hand and she listened speechless as Keith Higgins, Steve's boss explained what had happened at work.

When Sally managed to explain that she had not heard anything from Steve, Keith sounded concerned.

Ten minutes later, the office phone rang again. Sally had ignored it twice already.

This time she picked it up.

She listened, and, a few moments later, she hung up.

Chapter 40

The book sat in front of him, the whiteness of the room hurting his eyes. He could see the table. On it was the book, its cover in white. Again, he could feel no air, but the cover opened. He could see the pages turning from right to left. Every page had writing on it, but nothing was coming into focus as the pages were turning. It began to slow down. He held his breath, not wanting anything to influence what was happening.

The pages stopped.

On the left-hand side, two lines slowly appeared from top to bottom.

He recognised the name; he had seen it before.

The date started to appear in front of him:

17/10.

In the third column: Falling.

The banging on the door got louder; it was aggressive, and he could hear someone shouting. He tried to look at the book again, but it had gone. Instead, he was gaining consciousness, looking around the room. The knocking on the door continued.

He now realised he was still in the hotel bedroom, a broken champagne flute lay on the bed alongside an empty bottle.

Steve slid carefully out of the bed as not to get glass on the floor, he called out to the person knocking the door to let them know he was on his way. Grabbing the dressing gown off the back of the door, he opened it.

The maid stood in front of him, her vacuum cleaner in one hand and towels in the other.

In a very broken English accent, the rather aggressive woman told Steve she needed to clean the room immediately.

Steve looked at his watch; it was 11:30.

Twenty minutes later, he was sitting in his car in the hotel car park and was reading the hotel bill.

He didn't remember ordering room service or the premium late-night film channel on TV. He paid the £387 and knew it was too late to dispute the bill. He had also outstayed his welcome. Checkout was at 10am.

Steve looked at his watch again: 12:20. Then he noticed the date. His heart missed a beat.

It was the 17th of October.

He closed his eyes and visualised the book; he could see the name again. It was as clear as day.

Chapter 41

A woman with a young child in a pushchair stood by the railings, her back to the road. She was crying uncontrollably. An older lady who had dropped her two Tesco carrier shopping bags had her arm around the woman. She was also looking over her shoulder at what was happening a few meters away from her.

A bus driver who happened to be driving in the opposite direction was now kneeling on the ground and a middle-aged man with fluorescent jacket and cement stained work trousers was next to him. There were other people around looking to see what was going on.

The woman with the pushchair was screaming. She could see the horrific scene, the images would last a lifetime.

Under the back wheels of the truck were the remains of a bicycle. It had been crumpled and almost folded in two; the front light was still on.

It wasn't showing the road ahead; now it was shining on the ground and reflecting a red pool. The truck had dragged the body for six meters. There was a distinct trail of blood behind it. The car behind was now stopped over the trail, the female driver still in the car. She was also crying hysterically and was being comforted by another woman who had been waiting to cross the road.

The man with the fluorescent jacket was the driver. His face was devoid of blood, and he vomited as he looked closer. The bus driver also turned away. He put his arm around the truck driver and started to heave as well.

The body, or what was left of it, was just a ball of sinew and so crumpled it did not resemble anything human.

What had shocked the two men the most was the look on the face of the poor guy. He had been wearing a bright orange ruck sack, the word FORD clearly visible. The man's chin was resting on the rucksack. Still wearing his cycle helmet, his head had been turned 180 degrees. His eyes were wide open and unfocused. It was as if he were in a trance. Unfortunately, Dean was not in a trance.

Eighteen cars behind the incident, Steve was sitting in his car. He wondered if there had been an accident or if it was roadworks. A moment later, he heard the sirens. He felt his body go cold, and he shivered. Looking in his rear view mirror, he could see a fire engine closely followed by an ambulance. They both safely passed him, but he could clearly see from a few cars in front of him that traffic was at a standstill.

The temptation to get out of his car was huge.

His breath became short, and it hurt to breathe in. His chest felt tight. He turned the air conditioning up as high and as cold as possible.

Steve was now gasping for air. He pressed the button to open his window but nothing happened. His head was spinning. He crossed his arms tightly over his chest and pulled them into his body as tight as possible. Now panicking, he pulled the lever to open his door. He flung it open, and, in doing so, almost knocked a young lad in a school uniform off his bicycle.

Steve stood as straight as he could. He briefly noticed the rear window of his car was open, which explained why his front window didn't work.

Moments later, he was looking past all the traffic he could see a sea of blue lights in the distance, and there was a crowd of people looking at something.

A uniformed policeman was walking towards him and asking drivers to get in their cars. Steve was aware that his breathing was back to normal.

"Please get into your car, sir; we will be asking everyone to turn around as the road ahead has now been closed," the constable demanded.

Steve asked what had happened and the reply was brief: "There has been an RTA."

All the traffic behind him had eventually been cleared, and it was Steve's turn to reverse his car into a bus stop to turn around. As he began to pull away, he looked across the road and recognised the woman standing in the queue for a bus. It was Mari.

He jammed on his brakes. Thankfully, the car behind him also came to a sudden halt. The driver pushed his horn so hard that is almost drowned Steve's voice as he called out to Mari.

It took him a few attempts to attract her attention. She looked at him for a moment before eventually leaving the bus stop and carefully crossing the road to Steve's car.

The man in the car behind was now shouting and using various sign language that was being ignored.

Steve leaned over to the passenger side of the car and opened the door, Mari sat in the passenger seat, and they drove off.

He pulled forward just as the irate driver behind was overtaking him. This caused him to swerve quickly to avoid a collision.

The man beside them took advantage of his horn once again. The driver now shouting and still using his comprehensive knowledge of sign language.

Steve suddenly turned left into a narrow street, leaving the driver of the other car no time to pursue. These were roads Steve knew well, and, a few moments later, he turned left, right, left, right and left again. Eventually, he came to a halt in a space outside a little terraced cottage.

Steve turned to Mari and apologised about his driving. "Mari is looking a little worried," he thought, but, despite what he thought, Mari was extremely pleased to see him.

As they drove the six or so miles towards the hospital, Steve told his passenger about losing his job and that he had been hoping to find her.

As they neared the hospital, they both agreed to meet after Mari's shift. She was due to finish at 11 pm.

Steve watched Mari walk away from him; for a second, he couldn't remember where he had put the cash he drew out of the bank.

He opened the glovebox of the car, and there, in front of him, was the remaining £9500. He breathed a huge sigh of relief.

He drove to the local shopping centre and brought himself a suitcase. He then went into two of his favourite stores. He had never spent so much money on clothes in his life; the bill in the Crew store was £1727, and, in Fat Face, he spent another £1500, plus another £1500 on a suit in the fancy Taylors.

Two hours later, he checked himself into the Travelodge motel nearest the hospital. Using the name Andy Burton, he checked in and collapsed on the bed. He switched the TV on as the local news came on.

Steve stood under the hot water for five minutes. On the TV news, the reporter was talking about the tragic accident where a cyclist, a local man, had been unfortunately killed when he was involved in a collision with a truck.

Feeling exhausted, Steve collapsed on the bed. He watched a report from the local flower show and fell asleep.

Three minutes later, another reporter signed in at the scene of the cyclist's accident.

Steve missed it.

Chapter 42

Debbie picked the phone up again.

"ACJ how can I help?"

The phone went dead again.

"Dickhead!" she shouted down the dead phone line.

Chapter 43

Sandra was sitting on her bed, finishing her cup of Fazenda Santas Ines coffee. She walked into the kitchen but not before stopping at the full-length mirror to admire her body. She blew herself a kiss.

Standing at the sink and looking out of the window, she caught a glimpse of the neighbour who's garden backed onto hers. She had been flashing him for months now and was enjoying the thought of him having fantasies about her. She stood at the sink, washing her mug for a lot longer than necessary. She was wearing her signature Fleur du Mal silk French knickers and a pair of washing up gloves. The man was in his shed, pretending to be busy but was looking directly in her direction.

She was just about to squeeze some soapsuds over her breasts when the phone rang.

She ripped off her yellow gloves, ran into the bedroom, sat on the edge of her bed and picked the phone up. "Hi," was the only thing she said. She listened intently before confirming the last thing that was said,

"So 11pm."

She hung up.

Chapter 44

Sally had been going out of her mind. She was now thinking something had happened to Steve. On the radio earlier, it was reported that a cyclist had been killed in town. For a moment, she had wondered if the cyclist was him.

Sally had already talked to Billington and confided in another of her colleagues in the office, asking them if she should call the police. She reluctantly decided to give him another twenty-four hours.

As much as Sally had tried to concentrate on her work, she had so much on her mind that she found it impossible.

Steve's disappearance was a significant inconvenience to her other business. She had received a call earlier in the day from a guy who had wanted to talk to her; he had a proposition which could make her a serious amount of money.

Sally called Billington straight away. They discussed the phone call but decided the timing was all wrong. They had to be patient until Steve came home or, at least, until they had heard from him.

Chapter 45

Steve woke and, for a second, thought he had overslept. He looked at his watch: 7 pm.

Laying back on the bed, he found the room service menu and ordered a Caesar salad and a portion of chips. He was even happier to see that San Miguel was also on the menu. He ordered a pint.

The meal arrived thirty minutes later, which took a lot less time to eat.

After another long shower, Steve lay on the bed to watch the TV. He was trying not to think about the accident that morning. His thoughts then turned to Sally, he felt guilty and upset at the same time. Sitting on the side of the bed, he picked the phone up and dialled the house phone. It rang, and rang, and rang. Finally, the answerphone cut in. It was her voice, which made him feel even worse. He hung up.

Chapter 46

Sally heard the house phone from the office. She couldn't run in and answer it, because she was on the other line. She was talking to her personal bank manager, regarding the £250k that had been put into her account. She had to move some money as soon as possible.

Sally knew the money from her father for the wedding had been taken out of Steve's account. She had received a call from the bank manager minutes after the money had been withdrawn. It was good to have contacts like hers. She could normally get what she wanted from most people. There was always a way, even if it did mean bending rules. As far as she was concerned, rules were there to be bent or broken if necessary.

Steve tried the house phone one more time, but there was no answer. He walked over to the small dressing table in the room and picked up the pencil and the hotel branded note pad.

He sat back on the bed and began writing.

Dream 1 = Patricia/died.

Dream 2 = Robert/missing.

Dream 3 = Alan/missing

Dream 4 = Dean/ today (17/10) fall

Then it hit him. The blood drained from his face, his heartbeat increased, and he began to feel nauseous. He grabbed the bottle of water sitting on the bedside cabinet; it was warm, but he gulped the contents down.

Staring at what was written in front of him, he was aware the room was moving as if he was drunk. "SHIT.

SHIT! SHIT! Oh no, what the fuck is happening to me, why me, why me?"

Steve stared at the page again.

Unsure what to do next, he just looked at the words. He could feel from deep inside his gut that the poor bastard under the truck was Dean. He didn't need to hear the news; he knew.

Picking the paper and pencil up, he wrote one more line.

22/03, me.

He circled the date so much the pencil tore through the paper.

"5 Months!" he said through gritted teeth. He cried.

The phone rang and, without thinking, he picked it up.

Steve didn't know what to say at first. With tears still in his eyes and needing to blow his nose, he sniffed as he heard her voice.

"Steve, I love you," she said.

"Whatever you have done, please talk to me. Let's work this out together."

Sally could tell he was crying; he didn't say a word. He didn't need to.

"Please listen to me; we need to talk. I need to talk to you, please."

She continued and all he could do was listen.

"Sweetheart, I know about the money. I don't care, I don't care if you have spent it. I know about work, and I know what happened to Dean this morning."

The last eight words hit him hard. Sally could hear him sobbing.

"I'm so sorry," Sally said.

"Are you sure it was Dean?" Steve's voice was almost incomprehensible.

Sally explained that Keith had phoned her, because he had received a message from him about the car. Keith wanted to know if the two of them had spoken. Keith then told Sally that Dean tried to undertake the truck, which he didn't realise was turning left. His sister-in-law and her young daughter were very close, and they had seen everything.

Steve told Sally about the dream; he had seen Deans name, today's date, and the word "fall".

The two of them sat silently. It was Sally who spoke first. She asked him if they could meet. It didn't matter where, but they needed to talk. They both agreed to meet at the cottage at 11 am the following morning.

Still sitting on the bed, Steve picked up the piece of paper again.

Suddenly a feeling of guilt hit him; he had seen Deans name in a dream Why was he was seeing the book, and could he see more?

There were so many questions now going around in his head that he needed to talk to someone. He knew he couldn't talk to Sally about the dreams he had of her parents. How could he approach that subject now?

Was this all coincidence? That thought was dismissed almost immediately when he remembered the night Patricia had died; he woke at 12:03, the exact time she died. He then dreams about Dean, two about the poor sod; he may have had two chances of saving his life.

Steve picked the note pad and pencil up.

He turned the pad over, so he had a whole page to write on. Starting at the top of the page, he wrote:

Make love to Mari.
Drive as fast as possible.
Buy a new bike.
4-Holiday . . . Italy, Corfu, VEGA$$$$$$$
5-Buy a boat.
6-Tell Sally the truth (or most of it)
7-
8-
9-
10-

He left 7-10 blank, because he noticed the time.

The bucket list had to wait. He had five months to complete the list.

Getting off the bed and walking towards the bathroom, Steve stopped, turned around, and walked back to the bed. He picked the list up and crossed out number six.

Chapter 47

The evening shift at the hospital could be quite unpredictable.

Mari had been a general nurse for many years, and she loved her job. It was the unpredictability of the work that she loved; no two days were the same, and tonight's shift was thankfully quieter than normal. The ward on which she was working consisted mainly of short-term patients; most of them were in because of some kind or minor trauma or for routine surgery where an overnight stay was required. The only person of concern on this shift was an elderly man with a broken hip. He was fast asleep, but his snoring was disturbing other patients.

Mari had been thinking about Steve all afternoon. She liked him and was feeling uncomfortable about the phone call she had made earlier that day.

The money she had been offered would be such a help; she was sending a large percentage of her wages home to her father in Corfu. The family had owed money in taxes, and her father could not work any longer due to bad health. It was her responsibility to look after him now, especially since the accident in which her brothers had died.

Mari had done the maths; she could pay all the of taxes off and put a deposit down on an apartment in Messonghi where her father lived and where she was born.

All she needed to do was to help her best friend, the girl that had helped get her work, the girl who had paid for the flight to England. She owed so much to Sandra.

Chapter 48

Debbie looked at the clock on her office wall.

It was 8pm, an hour later than her usual time to leave. She hated locking the business up on her own. As she switched the office lights off, she noticed a light on in the boardroom.

To get to the room Debbie had to walk through the vast industrial unit and up the steel staircase. She hated the steps as they were steep and often very dirty. She decided to forget the light, and, after checking the warehouse doors, she punched the code into the alarm pad by the main door.

The alarm beeped four times and went quiet.

She tried again, and the same thing happened.

The only reason for the alarm not working was because one of the trigger sensors on one of the doors may not be lined up. There was no other option; she had to check them all.

Debbie always carried a torch in her bag when it was dark. The torch was also a weapon, and, if someone decided to attack her, she could use it to defend herself. She was very capable of doing that. One of her hobbies was self-defence, and she had attended classes for over a year.

Having switched the torch on, she checked her door first, then, one by one, she looked at the massive roller doors in the unit. All four were secure. It left one option; the Board Room where the light was on.

Walking slowly across the concrete floor, she nearly tripped over a lonesome wooden pallet that had been left by one of the drivers. She made a mental note of it so she could have a word with the guys in the morning. Shining the very bright light beam up the stairs, she began to climb up. Being very careful not to slip on the steps, she was almost halfway when she heard a raised voice.

She switched the torch off and opened her mouth so she couldn't hear her breath. It was quiet for a while. A moment later, she heard a voice she recognised. It was one of the directors of the business, and he sounded agitated.

As much as she tried, she couldn't make out the words. One step at a time, in the pitch darkness, she climbed the steps.

There were three more steps to get to the top. She stood as quiet as she could, straining to hear. It went silent.

A few seconds later, the door burst open. It swung outwards and hit something behind it hard, the glass in the door shattered. Fragments of sharp glass fell on the wood floor breaking again into smaller pieces. The sound echoed inside the industrial unit, and Debbie froze.

Standing in the doorway looking as if he was going to kill her stood Pete. He was over six foot tall and a mass of a man. His bulk stood in front of the poor woman who looked petrified. Debbie, for a moment, thought he was going to throw her down the stairs. Then it went quiet.

Pete looked at Debbie's pale face, and he could see how frightened she was. A moment later, Pete's face changed; he could now see tears rolling down Debbie's face and his persona changed. He began to apologise and took a step towards her.

As much as she wanted to run down the stairs, Debbie was frozen to the spot. She stood rigid, still terrified and afraid to move. She stared at the bulk in front of her.

Pete stood on the top step, still apologising.

"What are you doing here Debbie"? Pete asked.

She took a deep breath and explained that she had worked late, and that the alarm wouldn't set, so she was checking the doors when she heard him.

Pete looked very sorry for scaring her; he held out his hand and apologised again.

"Come with me; I need to show you something," he said.

Again, he held out his huge hand; reluctantly, Debbie took two more steps up before she placed her hand into his. Being very careful to avoid the glass on the floor, she stood on the landing. Stepping over the final shards of glass, she followed Pete's lead into the board room.

The room was well lit; huge lights hung from the false ceiling, and the massive table sat in front of her. There were four chairs on each side and, at the head of the table, was the chairman's seat.

Debbie's heart stopped.

Alan looked at Debbie, and he had a huge smile on his face. The missing man was sitting in front of her. She was momentarily speechless.

All he said was,

"Hello Debbie."

Chapter 49

Relieved that he was going to see Sally, Steve was thinking about what he was going to say. He knew he would upset Sally, but he had no choice.

Looking at himself in the mirror, he admired his new clothes and checked the new shoes to make sure he had removed the sale stickers from the soles.

In the inside pocket of the smart jacket, he had a thousand pounds in cash. "That should be enough for the night," he hoped.

Standing in the foyer of the motel, Steve checked the time on his watch: 10:30.

At 10:33, a new Mercedes 200 saloon pulled up. The driver got out and walked into the motel.

At 10:45, all of Steve's bags and the new case were in the boot of the rented car. Steve sat in the driver's seat and drove out of the car park.

The drive to the hospital took him six minutes. He parked the car and walked the hundred meeters to the large entrance.

It was 11 pm exactly. Seven agonising minutes later, Mari walked towards him. Relieved he had not been stood up, Steve smiled; he was now beginning to think this was the start of something special.

Mari saw Steve waiting and, for a moment, had to do a double take. She thought he looked extremely smart and very handsome. As she walked toward him, she again felt sorry for him. He was going to be used. She had instructions from Sandra, and all she needed to do was to get him to fall for her at this stage. She had to do whatever it took, and she meant whatever.

Steve had booked the Hilton in Bournemouth, their King one-bedroom suite with a sea view.

Neither of them noticed the brand-new silver Audi RS4 that was following them.

Mari had not planned to stay the night with Steve. She was wearing her nurses uniform and didn't even have a clean pair of knickers with her. She turned to Steve and asked him if he would take her to her apartment so she could get changed. The answer shocked her; Steve said he had been shopping and brought her something to wear.

Mari didn't say anything; she just smiled at Steve and thanked him. She wondered for a moment if she was safe. She had heard about one of the other nurses at the hospital who had been abducted, raped, and dumped in skip. She didn't know if it was true, but it had shocked her.

Sally soaked in the bath; she shaved her legs and tidied what she called her happy trail. She was so pleased at last to have spoken to Steve, and she was looking forward to seeing him the following day.

After the bath, she showered, washing her hair and conditioning it. She was very proud of her body, and, although she had put some weight on in the last few weeks, she loved her delete her curves.

She dried herself off in the bedroom and used hair straighteners to perfect the look.

Her white blouse sat on the bed and next to it was a short black skirt and a pair of black sheer tights. She decided not to wear any knickers, it made her feel free and she loved the feeling of the tights against her pussy.

She sat on the sofa in the lounge of the cosy cottage. The log burner was on. It had been a lovely day and the evenings were getting cooler. There was a frost predicted, so the fire warmed the cottage perfectly. There was a large glass of white wine sitting on the coffee table with half the bottle gone already.

The silver Audi TT pulled up on the driveway.

Chapter 50

Debbie sat in the chair next to Alan while Pete was sweeping the broken glass into a pile.

The poor girl wasn't sure if she was going to cry or if she should jump over the table and kiss him.

She waited, quietly looking at the man she thought was dead to hear what he had to say.

"Debbie, I can't apologise enough; you weren't supposed to see me, and, unfortunately, being here implicates you. Pete and James are the only two people who know the truth. It's all my doing.

I'm afraid I've got myself into a bit of bother and the only way I could deal with it is to go missing. I've worked so hard to build this business up and I'm so sorry."

Alan paused. There were tears in his eyes, and Debbie wanted to hold him, to tell him that everything would be all right.

He continued,

"You don't need to know everything, but I did a job for someone, and, unfortunately, things didn't quite go the way they should have.

The only way I could get out of this would be to sell the business or . . ."

Pete walked over and sat on the table. He pulled the chair up and placed his feet on it.

Debbie looked at the man. He used to be a body builder, and, although he still went to the gym most days, he didn't compete like he used to. His body towered over Debbie, but she knew he had a heart of gold and wouldn't hurt her.

It was Pete who spoke next in his lovely, coarse London accent

"Debbie, Alan's sparing you the 'ard stuff. If 'e weren't gonna sell ACJ to pay wot 'e owed 'e woz gonna be proppin up a . . ."

Alan stopped Pete from saying any more.

He then continued to tell Debbie that he had been paying himself more than he was owed. He had also been paying his two directors more as well. The three of them were investing money through a broker.

Debbie had already worked out for herself that the two names on the payroll were possibly backhanders, but she had no idea Alan would have gotten involved in something like this.

Innocently, Debbie suggested Alan go to the police. He sat in the big chair and smiled at her.

He explained that, apart from going to prison for fraud, the business would possibly fold and, more than likely, the people he owed money to would find a way of getting to him.

Then Debbie's world fell apart.

"I'm so sorry, love. I can't have you involved in this. I need you to resign from ACJ."

The words echoed in her head, staying on to work an extra hour for the company she loved was now going to cost her her career.

Tears rolled down Debbie's cheeks.

She could not believe what she was hearing. She stood up and started to argue her case. She told Alan she suspected fraudulent bookkeeping. She had kept quiet, not telling a soul, and when the police were going through ACJs finances, she had acted in the company's best interest.

The three of them sat in silence. Alan was thinking about what Debbie had just said. He couldn't argue with her. In his absence, ACJ was going from strength to strength.

The poor woman had so many questions to ask. She loved the man, and she would do anything for him. He just didn't know it.

Two hours later, Debbie sat in her car, tears again rolling down her cheeks. She felt sick with worry, and she still didn't know if she had a job to go to in the morning.

Chapter 51

The Audi sat outside the Hilton. Inside it, Sandra sat in total darkness, wondering how things were going. She thought about going up to the Sky Bar in the hotel; she wanted a drink, and the view from the top of the hotel was simply amazing. You could see for miles, and it was also a fantastic place to meet business men in need of some company.

She smiled to herself and remembered meeting a very drunk lawyer who was in Bournemouth defending a local man involved in some kind of money laundering case. She had met him in the bar and, within two hours, had managed to get him into his room. She did her signature strip in front of him, and he passed out. Thankfully, he had paid her before she got undressed. That was a good night.

Starting the car up, she decided to go home. She loved the sound of her car; the V8 burbled as if it were talking to her. The tires howled as she floored the accelerator. Looking in the rear view mirror, she could see plumes of smoke pouring out from the wheel arches. Moments later, she switched the traction control back on. She had palpitations and felt light headed, wondering if it were possible to have an orgasm by driving quickly. She vowed to try but not tonight.

Chapter 52

The room was exactly how he had hoped. There was an ice bucket with a bottle of champagne next to the bed and a large bouquet of flowers on the side. The bellboy waited for his tip with a big smile. Mari walked in first without saying a word; she walked into the bathroom and left the door open just enough for someone to be able to watch her without being obvious.

Steve put his hand into his pocket and handed the young man a note. At the last moment, he saw he had handed over £50 by mistake. Realising it was too late, he smiled as the bellboy retreated into the hallway thanking his best customer of the evening.

Steve could hear the shower, but, rather than spoil the surprise, he did the gentlemanly thing and left her to it.

Mari walked back into the room just as Steve was opening his suitcase. He took out a large flat box and three smaller gift-wrapped parcels. He lay them on the bed and stepped back.

He looked at her as she stood in front of him. She had a brilliant white Egyptian towel wrapped around her. Her hair was wet but looked perfect.

"Blue box first," he told her.

Mari pulled the ribbon off the box and let it fall to the floor. Opening it slowly, she removed the bright pink tissue paper and picked out the expensive Fleur du Mal silk panties.

Mari smiled as she held them up and blew him a kiss. What she didn't say to him was that she recognised the panties; she knew how much they cost, and she also knew who else loved them.

In the largest box was the most beautiful dress. The label said "Karen Millen" and the fabric was the whitest she had

ever seen. It was a simple, classic design, and she held up against herself as she looked in the mirror.

It was cut above her knee. She was worried that the top half would be too large for her small boobs. Again, she smiled at Steve who was holding the last box. She recognised the logo on the box and opened it with excitement. She pulled out a pair of white Jimmy Choo high-heeled Hologram mesh booties. Words failed her for a moment, and her eyes filled with tears of joy.

Putting the shoes back in the box, she walked over to Steve and put her arms around him. She kissed him on the cheek first, and, then looking into his eyes, she pushed her lips against his.

Still holding on to her towel she picked up all three boxes and walked back into the bathroom. She shut the door, carefully placing all the boxes on the toilet seat. She took her towel off and sat naked on the edge of the corner bath. She used the towel to hide her sobbing.

Ten minutes later, the bathroom door opened. Mari walked into the bedroom. She looked stunning; the dress fitted her perfectly. Her hair was now dry and perfectly styled, and her Greek skin bronzed body glowed. She had never worn makeup, and, luckily for her, she didn't need it.

The waistline of the dress enhanced her athletic build, and the sexiest of booties complimented the look.

Steve felt quite under dressed despite wearing a new Armani white shirt a black tie and a suit he picked up earlier from Brook Taverner.

The two of them admired each other for a moment before Steve held out his hand. He led his stunning date out and to the lift. During dinner, Mari listened to Steve as if it were the last conversation she would ever hear.

He told her all about the dreams, about the night he woke at 12.03, about Sally, and about Sally's mother. He felt as if the whole world had been weighing him down; he felt as if he could tell her anything.

Mari listened intently when he told her that he knew Sally was having affairs and that she had special friends that visited the cottage they shared. Steve kept two things to himself; one was finding the picture of Billington and the other woman he now knew was Sandra, and the second was the dream about the 22nd of March with his name.

It was during the dessert course that Steve started asking Mari more about her and her family. He was very keen to know about Corfu. Steve couldn't believe his luck when he found out Mari's uncle Costas was a marine broker; he sold boats and ships all around the world, and he had also supplied yachts to a very well-known American actor who regularly visited the island.

Steve also kept quiet about his bucket list but had already worked out that three of the ten things involved the beautiful creature in front of him.

Why the amazing, beautiful, stunning woman was interested in him, he had no idea, but he was hoping she would make him the happiest man in the world for the limited time he had left.

Chapter 53

Sandra sat on her bed, wearing her favourite pair of striped pyjamas. She brought them for a pyjama party, which she remembered fondly. It was a shared house warming party at Sally's, and there were six very drunk ladies, all wearing their night wear. Sandra looked at the pyjama top and the second button was still missing from where her top had been ripped off her.

She smiled to herself. She took a sip of her expensive coffee and looked at the three envelopes in front of her. They all had names on them.

She opened the first envelope and tipped the contents out on the bed; all the pictures were of the same girl. Looking at each picture in fine detail, Sandra put them one by one in one of three piles: yes, no, and maybe.

She then did the same with the next two envelopes; eventually, she had a pile of thirty definite, fifty maybes, and 130 for the shredder. She went through the maybe pile again, and took twenty out.

She put them in a new envelope, and, with a marker pen, she wrote on the envelope a single word: "Safe".

Chapter 54

Steve swiped the card into the room handle. With a faint plip and a green light, he heard the door unlock. He opened the door a little, and Mari entered the room in front of him.

The room was stifling hot. Mari walked over to the balcony door and slid it open. The air was cold, but it was comfortable. The sound of the traffic ten stories below and a distant police siren could be heard, but it was the sound of the waves breaking gently on Bournemouth beach that reminded her of the beauty in nature.

Mari took the lead; she turned to Steve, and, wrapping her arms around him, she kissed him. The kiss felt different, more tender and with feeling. They both closed their eyes and savoured the moment.

Steve wished he had seen this moment in his dream. Dying of happiness, he would accept that gratefully.

Mari shivered, so Steve took her hand and led her inside, sliding the door shut behind him.

Mari sat on the end of the bed in front of him as he removed his jacket and tie and stood, looking at her.

"Mari, I have decided that I need to change my life. There are things I want to do, and there are places I want to go. More importantly, I want you to come with me."

Mari was trying to process this; this was not part of the plan, but in this moment in time, she felt happier than she could have ever imagined. She told Steve she needed time to sort things out. "Maybe we could go to Corfu for a holiday," she said.

Rather than spoil the moment, Steve agreed.

Mari stood up and stepped closer to Steve. She put her arms around his neck and looked into his eyes. She could feel the hurt inside him and wanted to make things better.

As they kissed, their thoughts were not entirely in tune with each other.

In his mind, he was trying to keep calm. He was trying to plan what his next move should be. Should he stand back and start undoing his trousers? Should he undo her dress? Should he drop to his knees? All these thoughts circled his mind.

In her mind, she was trying to work out if she should tell him about Sandra and her relationship. He should know what kind of woman he had been living with. She didn't want to spoil the evening. He did not deserve that. Eventually, it was her who made the first move.

She stepped back, reached behind her, and pulled the thin strip of material, which was hanging in between her shoulder blades. She felt the dress release its hold on her breasts. She smiled as the dress slipped off her. She was still wearing the beautiful panties and the sexiest booties she had ever seen.

Mari had always taken good care of her body, using the best lotions she could afford. She used the local gym and ran nearly every day. She knew it was worth the pain. The look on Steve's face gave her goose pimples; she was offering herself to him and wanted him so much. Even before he touched her, she could feel herself getting wet.

Steve looked at Mari's stunning figure. "So perfect," he thought. "Sheer perfection."

As she turned her back on him, he prayed she had no tattoos, especially one of a black cat. He need not have worried as Mari would never deface or decorate her body. Putting his hands on her hips, he took a small step towards her. His body pressed against hers, he could feel the heat radiating against him.

Mari reached behind her. She could already feel the bulge against her bottom. She fumbled to undo Steve's belt, so he took over, removing it completely. He quickly undid the button and zip, his trousers fell to the floor, and he clumsily kicked off his shoes. One of them flew across the room and hit the ice bucket. Thankfully, it didn't fall over, but it did make Mari giggle as she realised what the clang was.

Trousers followed a similar route across the room and slid under the writing desk. He decided not to launch his now very tight-fitting classic trunks but slipped them off and kicked them gently under the bed.

Mari was leaning forward over the bed in front of him with her hands on the bed covers. She looked over her shoulder and smiled.

Steve left the very expensive panties in place, he couldn't help smiling as he looked at her, her beautiful bottom covered in the most expensive silk and the little booties added to his excitement. He pulled the gusset of her panties to one side. Her perfection was more than skin deep.

Mari used her hand between her legs to guide him inside her. Her head started to spin, and her first orgasm made her shudder. The intense heat from her body making her face feel flushed, she continued to look into his eyes. They were dancing between watching himself sliding in and out of her pussy and her eyes. She bit her lower lip as her second orgasm approached.

As the sun breached the horizon on the new day, the two of them lay in bed without saying a word. Mari was laying on her back now naked. Steve was on his side running his hands up and down her body, the two of them more contented than they could have ever imagined.

They fell asleep again until the phone in the room rang waking them. Mari answered it and the two of them were brought to earth with a bump. They were given 15 minutes to vacate the room. Mari was due at the hospital in 3 hours, and Steve was due at the cottage in less than 30 minutes. He would be late.

Chapter 55

Sally woke at 5am. She was going over things in her mind and working out how much Steve really needed to know, it was going to be a calculated discussion and she was going to be in control.

The hired Mercedes pulled onto the cottage drive at 11:45. Having had a very quick shower at Mari's hotel room, he changed into a new pair of jeans and his now favourite Fat Face sweatshirt, he finished the look with his 10 year old trainers which he still liked wearing, Sally hated them.

The open stable door was at the rear of the cottage, the radio was on in the kitchen and as he walked in Steve could see the log burner in the lounge was lit, he instantly thought about the wasted heat in the room until he saw Sally sitting on the sofa.

In a split-second Sally turned on him.

The calm calculated discussion was already a distant memory.

Sally walked up to Steve and raised her hand to him, she didn't strike the blow but soon wished she had, instead she just turned her back and sat back down on the sofa, she crossed her arms and wondered what had happened to the man she used to know.

He looked different, he was looking smarter than she had remembered, he almost looked smug, this pissed her off even more.

Steve sat in what was his favourite chair and looked at Sally, he wanted to hear the truth and he also wanted to tell her the truth, but that wasn't going to happen.

She spoke first asking him what was going on, she wanted to know if he was coming home.

Steve replied,

"You remember the dreams I have." Sally stood up and stopped him from saying any more, she was keen to control the conversation

but was struggling to do so. "What do you want Steve?" she asked. As she sat down, Steve stood, this also upset her, he was now in a higher position to her, a position of authority.

He then took control of the conversation.

"I don't expect you to understand what I'm going through" he began.

"The dreams I have had, I've had more. I knew . . ."

He paused to wonder for a moment how much he should tell Sally, given more time he could have thought things through, on this occasion his choice of words were going to have quite an impact.

"I'm sorry," he continued.

Then he told her things he regretted saying,

"I woke up at the exact time your mum died.

I saw your dads name in the book.

And I saw Alan's name, I knew Dean was going to die and . . ."

Tears were rolling down Sally's face now, but she sat silently listening, trying to let what she had just heard sink in.

"I've had another dream." Sally could see tears in his eyes.

"I dreamt" he paused, Sally was looking at him and she guessed what was coming.

"I dreamt that I saw my name, and I know when I am going to die."

Sally stood up and walked towards Steve, he pulled away from her which surprised her.

He sat down and waited for the barrage of questions.

"Why didn't you tell me about mum and dad?

What has happened to us Steve?" she asked.

"I'm so sorry but there are things I need to do; I love you but if I am going to die, there are places I want to visit and . . ."

Sally interrupted, "When did you become so selfish?"

Steve took this as an opportunity to approach a delicate subject, he continued.

"When did we start hiding things from each other?"

Sally looked at him unsure where this conversation was going, she didn't need to wait long.

"I know about your affairs, I've known for years. You do a good job at hiding things but not good enough. I knew you were different when I met you. I loved the unpredictability, but you are trying to live two lives."

Steve paused to find the right words, but he had gone too far now. He spoke his mind; he had nothing to lose so he continued.

"And, I knew you liked girls when we were younger. I thought it was just a phase. Did you know that Sandra called me after her birthday party the night we got back together?"

Sally didn't say a word.

"Sandra called me, she told me you went around to her apartment the day after, and she told me you had sex.

I thought so much about if I should say something. I wish I had, but I didn't. I kept quiet, and its eaten away at me for years. Now? Now it's gone too far. I don't know what you are involved in Sally, but I don't want to be a part of it.

I'm leaving you. I don't have long; I know when I am going to die, and I fully intend to make the most of my time left on this planet."

Steve walked into the kitchen, opened the fridge, and was pleased to see a bottle of his beer still sitting in the door. He opened the bottle and poured it into a glass. He stood in the kitchen drinking it when Sally walked in.

"I guess I owe you an apology, and I am sorry for not telling you things. You have always been so wrapped up in your own little world, I didn't think you noticed me some days. Yes, I did have a relationship with Sandra."

Sally was about to say she wasn't seeing her any longer, but what was the point of lying any further?

Steve listened to her side of the story.

"I don't know where we went wrong; I'm sorry. I wish I had told you about Sandra before. I've always known I liked girls, but I'm not a lesbian. I loved it when you held me, and when we had sex, it was fantastic. We have a beautiful house and money in the bank."

125

She hesitated because she didn't want to talk about the money. Steve finished his beer, rinsed the glass out in the sink, and put it on the drainer. He turned to Sally. "How would you feel if you were told you were going to die? What would you do? I know you won't give up what you have here, your job and the house." Steve's eyes filled with tears as he continued, "I need to just go, do what I need to do and live the rest of my life, hopefully with no lies. I love you sweetheart. I always will, but let me go. Live your life and do what you do best."

Steve took one last look at her and walked out of the kitchen and along the path to the driveway.

It wasn't often that Sally regretted something. As she hurled the rock over the garden fence at the Mercedes, this was one of those moments.

Steve saw the rock coming towards him and instinct told him to close his eyes.

The rock hit the middle of the windscreen. The noise inside the car was far louder than outside. The screen cracked from top to the bottom, although shocked Steve carried on driving. He compared the sound to a cowboy's whip but without an echo. He was pleased that he would only need to pay £50 excess on the insurance for a windscreen; it could have been ten times that if the rock had hit the car paintwork.

Chapter 56

Sally opened the office door at 3 pm; Steve had just left. She wanted to talk to Billington, but she had gone to a wedding in Paris.

A minute later, the office phone rang. She answered the call immediately; it was Sandra, and she sounded drunk.

She told Sally that Billington had gone away and wouldn't be back and said Sally had ruined her life. At the end of the call, she asked if Steve had always preferred doggy position, then hung up.

Sally sat behind her desk crying. Why was Sandra doing this to her? Sally reached up to the shelf that contained the box files. As she pulled the NHS Bournemouth file down and opened it, she tipped the contents of the file on to her desk and looked at the photos. She was thankful she had all the negatives.

Picking up the phone, she dialled Billington's number.

Chapter 57

Steve was driving back to Boscombe. Mari had given him her key and agreed he could stay with her a few days until he found somewhere more permanent.

As he approached the seafront at Southbourne, the fuel light came on. He was seconds away from the garage, so he pulled in.

Outside the kiosk sat a row of clear fronted newspaper racks, all the days daily papers were clearly on show and most of the covers were reporting on the abnormally mild weather and the usual political dribble. Steve smiled as one of them caught his eye; apparently, we are all descendants of Genghis Kahn.

But then he did a double take at the local paper; the headline on the Bournemouth Echo said,

"Local Businessman Arrested for Insurance Fraud."

Next to the headline was a picture of Alan.

Steve took the paper out of the rack and took it inside with him. He read more while waiting in the queue to pay for his fuel.

He read the first two lines before the cashier called to him. He quickly paid for his fuel and returned to his car.

He read the first two lines again, and this time he was interrupted by the car behind him pressing the horn in order to get to the pump.

A few minutes later, Steve pulled up outside Mari's place. She lived in the basement apartment in an avenue of large

Victorian houses most of which had been converted into apartments.

He sat on the small sofa and read the article.

"Local business owner, Alan Clive Jacobs, who owns ACJ Logistics, handed himself into Hampshire County Constabulary yesterday evening. Jacobs had been missing since 28th of September after picking a new yacht up from St. Peter Port Guernsey.

The yacht was found drifting off the Island on the morning of 29th with no sign of life on board. Guernsey RNLI, Air Sea Rescue, and The Chanel Island Police began searching the area immediately, and the hunt for Mr. Jacobs was officially called off three days later.

Jacobs, who the Echo believes owns properties in Southampton and in Kent, is to be held in custody until his trial in December. Although insurance fraud is suspected, we are unable to confirm this. We were also unable to get any comments from staff at ACJ at time of going to press."

Steve read the article three more times.

He lay on the bed and closed his eyes. The lack of sleep and a thumping headache made him feel ill. He kept on thinking about the dream. The date was right. Does this mean the dreams could be wrong? But what about Dean? He saw Dean's name twice, didn't he?

It was Mari that woke him. She had tried to be quiet when she opened the door, but Steve heard her key in the lock.

She was very happy to see the man lying on her bed. She wanted to jump on him but, like him, was suffering from a lack of sleep and wanted to get into bed as soon as possible. It was nearly midnight, and her next shift began in 8 hours. Ten minutes later, they lay in bed, and both fell asleep while holding each other.

Chapter 58

It was 4 am. Sandra was sitting up in bed. Despite it being October, she felt sticky. Slipping out of bed and walking over to the window, she opened her curtains and window. A slight breeze bellowed the curtains, which instantly cooled her down. She looked out into the darkness and could see the roof of her new car in the driveway. The street lamp reflected on the silver roof. She hated the colour. If she had chosen it, she would have asked for it to be white.

She got back into bed and reached across to her laptop that was still on. The screen lit her face as she looked at the numbers in front of her.

Chapter 59

Mari had already had a shower and was dressed in her uniform. She took great pride in what she wore and made sure she had a freshly pressed nurse's gown every day. Her comfy, patent black shoes freshly polished showed that she cared about her appearance and reflected her professional status.

Steve opened his eyes and smiled at her; she was beautiful and looking at her made him forget the bad things happening in his life.

He offered to take her in the car, but she said the bus was due in four minutes. She kissed his forehead and reminded him she was on a twelve hour shift. As she walked out of the door, she turned to him and blew him a kiss, which he caught in his hand and placed it on his cheek. She shut the door behind her.

Mari sat on the bus, looking out of the window. It was the first frosty morning, and she loved this time of year. It was cooler, and it made her think of her beloved Corfu. She adored the island and couldn't wait to return. She thought that she and Steve could go out there in May. She made a mental note to herself to check the flights at lunch time.

The bus stopped at the hospital, but Mari stayed on it; she was going to get off in three more stops.

Chapter 60

Debbie sat at her desk. The phone rang, and Pete asked her up to the board room.

As she got to the top of the stairs, she was glad to see the window had been fixed in the door. Through the opaque glass, she could see figures in the room. She knocked on the glass, and one of the figures moved towards the door and opened it. She was greeted by a female police officer in uniform.

She walked into the room and spotted Pete standing in front of her. Pete gave her a nervous smile. A very overweight man introduced himself as Detective Inspector Jake Evans and said he wanted to ask her some questions. Sandra sat in the nearest chair, and her heart felt as if it were going to burst through her chest. Her mouth felt dry, and, noticing her nerves, the female officer offered Sandra a drink of water, which she gladly accepted.

"Thank you, Sandra. Do you mind if I call you Sandra?" the detective asked. He didn't wait for a reply but continued,

"We are here to talk about your boss, Alan Jacobs. You are not in trouble; we need to clarify a few details about his disappearance and obviously his reappearance.

Alan has been very cooperative, and we need to clarify a few details." Sandra drank the cup of water and listened to the man now sitting in the chair next to her; his breath was rancid, a combination of Whisky, cigarettes, and garlic. Sally closed her nose and breathed through her mouth.

"Alan has told us about seeing you here in this room two evenings ago, and, to be honest, we are grateful to you, Sandra. If you hadn't walked into this room, he would have still been on the missing list."

Sandra couldn't believe what she was hearing.

"We need to ask you a few questions."

Pete looked at her, and he was smiling at her as if to say things were all ok.

"Did you know that Mr. Jacobs had decided to . . ."

There was a long pause then he rephrased the question.

"How did you feel when Mr. Jacobs went missing?"

Clearing her throat, Sandra spoke. There were tears in her eyes, and she was scared that she was going to say something she shouldn't.

"Alan is a good man, he is kind, funny, and has worked hard to build this business up. I took the phone call from Guernsey police asking about Alan. I couldn't believe it; I had no idea he wanted a bloody boat. He told me two days before he left.

It was the 26th of September, I'm really good at remembering dates." The detective thanked her for her help and said they would be in touch if they needed her any further. He shuffled his bulk off the desk, walked over to the door, and opened it for Sandra. He shut the door behind her as she carefully walked down the steel staircase.

Thirty minutes later, Pete walked into her office, and he closed the door behind him.

"I'm going to the police station to make a statement. If I'm not back by six and you leave, will you pop into mine and feed the cat, love?"

Sandra often used to do this. She drove past his house every day and loved to make a fuss of the manky old moggy as well.

As he opened the door, he looked at her and smiled.

"If things go ok. Alan will be in for a 5 stretch, out in two and a half."

He winked at her as he walked towards the waiting police officer.

The rest of her day was spent staring out of the window and hoping there wouldn't be another audit on the business accounts.

Chapter 61

Mari entered the swanky looking apartment block.

The apartment was purely a business premises as far as Sandra was concerned. It was also a fantastic investment; the apartment opposite hers sold recently for over a million pounds. It was also forty meters smaller and had no sea view.

The lift opened, and Mari pushed the door open. She closed it behind her and walked into the lounge. She loved walking into the apartment and vowed if she ever had enough money, she would live in a similar building.

Sandra was on the balcony, and she called out to Mari to join her. The view was spectacular. You could see the beach. There were only a handful of brave souls on the sand; some of them were walking on the sand while others were jogging or walking dogs.

In the distance, the Needle Rocks rose out of the choppy sea, sitting just off the west coast of the Isle of Wight. It was one of Mari's favourite views and made her think of her beloved Corfu.

Sandra put her arms around Mari and held her for a moment. She kissed her on her cheek and released her hold. The two of them walked into the lounge and sat on the vast white leather corner sofa.

Mari told Sandra everything she could remember. She told her of how she and Steve had made love. Sandra sat in silence, listening to every word. She had a big smile on her face.

Mari sat on the bus on its way to the hospital. She put her hand in her bag and felt the envelope containing £2000 cash. She was feeling guilty, guilty for telling Sandra about the sex and guilty for taking money. One thing she didn't tell her was that she loved the man she was betraying.

Chapter 62

Steve woke and looked at the bedside clock: it was 11:30 pm. He was covered in sweat. The sheets felt wet. Reaching between his legs, he checked to see if he had wet the bed. Relieved he hadn't, he threw the covers back. Holding his stomach, he could feel heat inside him rising. Although struggling to get out of bed, he staggered into the bathroom. Still naked, he got on to his knees put his hands on the toilet seat and lowered his head into the pan. He could smell lemon. Mari was an obsessive toilet cleaner; she used the liquid cleaner in the pan even if she had had a pee.

The feeling in his stomach got worse, and he began to heave. The first few times, he just choked. His eyes began to water, which he was thankful for when he started to vomit. Three times, the foul smelling fluid spewed out of his mouth. He struggled to catch his breath; just as he did, another wave of fluid poured into the bowl. His teeth felt dry, and his throat felt raw. It was burning. Struggling to stand, he reached behind him for the sink tap. Pulling himself up on the basin, he lowered his head and rinsed his mouth with the cold water. It relieved the burning for a moment; unfortunately, it was a very short moment. Steve tried to contain the bile inside his mouth until he was over the toilet. He didn't make it.

Almost coughing at the same time, the puke sprayed out of his mouth. He grabbed a towel from the rack behind him and held it up to his mouth until he was again over the toilet basin.

Still on his knees, he flushed the cistern for the umpteenth time. The vomiting had subsided. He pushed himself up and managed to sit on the toilet. The room was spinning; his stomach contents now flushed away, he tried to focus. Desperate to clean his teeth, he stood in front of the mirror, took hold of the toothpaste, and picked his brush up out of the mug on the shelf.

The convulsion was not like the others. He bent double, dropping the brush and paste, and his head made contact with the basin.

Moments later, Steve lay on the floor against the closed door in the bathroom. Blood was gushing from the wound on his forehead. His body lay crumpled like a rag doll, his breathing very shallow.

Chapter 63

The room seemed brighter. He was familiar with it now and seemed less inquisitive, feeling relaxed as if in a state of hypnosis. He looked at the white table. It was exactly as before; the white book with its cover still closed sat in the middle of the table. In his calm state, he could look around the room. There was nothing else in there with him. The walls, ceiling, and floor all so white, so bright. There was no door, just the walls. He was going to look to see how he got into the room but was suddenly aware of the book cover opening. He could see it perfectly. The pages began to turn; they were all blank. One by one, from right to left, they moved at the same speed, slow enough for him to notice if there was anything he could read.

The pages stopped. Both sides of the book were blank. Slowly the lines, one by one, from the top of the page to the bottom, two lines, three columns.

In the first column, the word "You" appeared.

Steve felt calm; he had seen this before. Then the date appeared; it just said "Today".

He waited for a moment; the third column was blank.

This was not like any other of the dreams he had. Steve felt at peace with what was in front of him, but then, as he looked back at the page again, the word "Today" began to fade.

Very slowly, letter by letter, the column was going blank. He looked closer. The "Y" was gone, then the "A", the "D", one by one. He was saying the letters to himself as they went.

Then the "O", and, lastly, the "T". He could now only see the word "You" on the left hand side of the page. He felt relieved. It felt as if a death sentence had been lifted, but as his relief set in and he looked around the room to find the exit, he took one last glance at the page.

You
22/03
Shot

There was a scream, a loud scream, an uncontrollable screaming piercing the calm.

Chapter 64

Sally sat at her desk, her computer in front of her. She was looking at the figures.

She now was beginning to wonder who she could trust. One of her options was to pack the car with a couple of cases and go.

She had a piece of A4 paper next to the keyboard. On the top she wrote "Go".

Halfway down the page, she wrote "Stay".

She remembered her father saying if in doubt always do a pros and cons list. Holding the pencil in her hand, she was ready to write.

Momentarily looking at the screen in front of her again, she began to cry.

Things had been so good; she had a good job, a loving partner, some very special friends, and now it was all going wrong.

The marine part of the business had been doing well. There were still lots of the usual divorce and house conveyancing work, but the juicy stuff had started to decline. As a partner, Sally had decided to reduce her hours. Mainly working from home suited her. It fitted in with her other interests, and she had contemplated giving up entirely, but she enjoyed the work.

Sally wished she had someone she could totally rely on.

Chapter 65

Steve knew he was in an ambulance; he had been sedated but recognised Mari sitting next to him and a paramedic standing over him.

He was so relaxed, aware of where he lay. He had a mask over his mouth, and the air he was breathing smelt like boiled sweets. He closed his eyes.

There were voices all around him. He couldn't open his eyes, and he heard a familiar voice telling him to relax and rest. Some of the words he recognised. A man said brain damage, another was talking about a scan. Steve knew he was in good hands. He took a deep breath, and everything went dark again.

Mari had no idea how long Steve had been on the floor. There was just enough room for her to get her head behind the door into the bathroom but she couldn't open it further. Steve was unconscious, and, seeing the dried blood on the floor, she knew enough to be very worried. She had run out into the street to get help; luckily, the guy who lived in the apartment above hers had heard the screams. He managed to push Steve away just enough for Mari to get through while her knight in shining armour called the ambulance.

Steve opened his eyes. He could see where he was. There was a tube in his mouth and another up his nose. As his eyes focused more, the machine next to him started making noises. Moments later, he could see the male nurse standing over him.

He had no idea that he had lost eight days, and it was eight days he could not afford to lose.

In a broken English accent, the nurse was telling Steve to relax, breath normally, and we will take the tube away. He also asked if Steve understood. He tried to nod but realised his head was being supported. With some effort, Steve raised his hand and stuck his thumb up.

A few minutes later, he seemed to be the centre of attention. The curtains were around the bed. With people all around him he knew he was in good hands.

The tubes started to disappear but not as fast as he hoped. An hour later, he was breathing on his own. Mari was now by his side, and two doctors were standing by the bed. One had already asked him questions (what day it was, his name, and the year). Both of them were concerned about his speech.

Mari leaned over the bed and kissed him, which made him smile. He tried to tell her he loved her. The words refused to leave his mouth. Mari could see how frustrated he was and stood up to talk to the doctors. Steve closed his eyes and thought to himself, "Today was not the day to die."

Chapter 66

Alan stood in court. His solicitor was in front of him and was pleased to be representing him. It wasn't going to be a difficult case. Alan had cooperated with the authorities and had pleaded guilty to insurance fraud. The policy he had taken out a few weeks prior to going missing was the one he hoped would save him. He later found out it was worthless, and the man who arranged it had himself gone missing. He was a rubbish fugitive; despite being in custody, Alan knew he was in Benalmadena, Spain and even knew the hotel he was staying in.

His appearance in court was to confirm his name, age, and address. The hearing was scheduled for the 8th of December. There was no application put in for bail, and Alan had accepted he had done wrong. He was willing to pay the price. He was going to be transferred to a remand centre until his trial.

Chapter 67

Steve woke early. He began to recite the alphabet. He could sense his voice was returning. He knew Mari was working on his ward that day and wanted his first words to her to be, "I love you".

There had been speculation that he had had a stroke, but one of the doctors insisted his brain injury was caused by him hitting the wash basin. The tests on the cause of his sickness were inconclusive. All Steve wanted was to start the journey he had been planning, the journey of a lifetime, the journey to end his life.

As Mari walked towards him, she could see the smile on his face. He was also in good voice. She lay next to him for a moment and held him; she knew she was getting her man back. Two hours later, the physio stood one side of him and Mari the other. The plan for the day was to get him out of the bed and into a wheelchair so he could get some fresh air in the garden and get to the bathroom.

You completely lose your dignity when a stranger has to wipe your bottom and place your penis into a cardboard bottle so you can have a pee. It's not something people think about, but when those two basic functions are taken away, you lose independence.

Laying on your back for long periods of time can have adverse effects on your body, along with the issue of not being able to have a relaxing crap. Your brain becomes used to being on the same level. It took a while to get Steve into his chair, which made him feel sick. It reminded him of his fall.

The nurse explained he may have vertigo as a side effect to his immobility over the last eight days.

Mari handed him a glass of water, which he gladly guzzled. It helped. Moments later, the wooziness eased off, and, with a blanket over him, Mari pushed him along the ward. This made Steve feel so much happier. Sitting in the garden together, the fresh October air felt amazing on his skin. He shivered once, and Mari stood to take him inside. Steve shook his head. He looked at her and clearly said, "No." He pulled his hands out from under the blanket and held onto the wheels of the wheelchair. He wanted to feel the cold; he loved to see the heat vapour leaving their mouths.

Sitting back down on the bench next to him, Mari turned and looked into Steve's eyes. She could see his frustration, and her heart felt heavy.

"We can do this" she said.

"I will look after you, and you will get better."

She was still looking at him, and he could see her eyes watering. She reached into her overall pocket, and, finding an old tissue, she wiped her eyes and smiled at him.

Mari stood up bent over and whispered in his ear, "I love you".

Those three words made all the difference. Steve had fallen in love with her from almost the moment they met. He had been asleep in the car at Boscombe beach. He often wondered why she had knocked on the window of his car, but right now he didn't care. He now had a good reason to live.

The bath was warm. Mari and the physio helped him in. He sat there like a child being bathed. They washed his hair, which felt amazing. The physio noticed that Steve was getting an erection. Medically, this was a very good sign. She asked Mari if it would be ok to go and have a coffee. She winked and smiled at Mari as she walked out of the bathroom and locked the door from the outside.

Steve lay exhausted in bed. He was relieved that at least one part of his body was in good form. Closing his eyes, it didn't take long for him to fall asleep.

At lunch time, Mari sat in the plush canteen, and, despite the massive choice of food on offer, she was picking through the Greek salad, which was covered in Feta Cheese.

She read the local newspaper that a colleague had left on the dining table, looking through the property section. She was trying to find a bigger apartment, one on the ground floor.

As Mari stood up to return her plate and cutlery, she closed the paper for the next person to read. She didn't see the picture and report on the front page.

"Local Businessman Dies".

The Bournemouth Echo can confirm that local businessman, Alan Jacobs, was found dead by prison officers yesterday afternoon.

The Echo spoke to an anonymous member staff who confirmed the story. The body of Mr. Jacobs was found in the bathroom at the remand centre where Jacobs had been awaiting trial for insurance fraud. The trial had been set for 8th of December. A full post-mortem is due to be held in the next few days.

Chapter 68

Sandra sat on the balcony of the vast Spanish villa, sipping coffee. She wished she had brought her own as it tasted nothing like hers.

Wearing the smallest of bikinis, it left very little to the imagination; she was hoping to get an all-over even tan.

She guessed the man sitting opposite her was around sixty years old, but it was difficult to tell. He needed a shave, and the sun was doing nothing for his bulbous red nose. His big cowboy hat hid his bald head, but she suspected that would also be very red.

He was wearing the biggest and thickest spectacles she had ever seen, which magnified his creepy little eyes.

The fat cigar ash fell onto his massive naked belly, making her feel sick.

He was on the phone talking in what she guessed was an eastern European language. It sounded to her like Polish.

Standing next to him was his fixer, dressed in a black business suit with a smart, white open shirt. Sandra could see he had a fantastic body. She flirted with him the previous day and almost got caught. She couldn't afford to upset things; she was going to try to keep this as a·business trip.

She had to address her host as Mr. G. She had no idea of his real name or very much about the man. All she cared about was getting the money for the photos she took with her and avoiding having to sleep with or kill the vile man.

Mr. G spoke on the phone for ages; eventually, he covered the mouthpiece and told Sandra to go for a swim. This pleased her. The pool was huge and cool. It was 34 degrees, and she needed to cool off. She grabbed her bag and walked down the steps to the pool. She turned to face the two men on the balcony and removed the small pieces of material that were covering her and began to apply tanning lotion to her body. She made the most of having an audience. She drizzled the tanning fluid over her breasts and took her time in rubbing it in. She then did the same to her recently enhanced bottom, giving the men something to dream about.

Chapter 69

Sally sat at her desk, looking out into the garden. There was a steaming cup of freshly ground coffee next to her; it filled the room with the sweetest aroma. She remembered when Steve used to blow her kisses while he cut the lawn and longed for those days to return.

Things were not going well for Sally; Billington had not been in contact since leaving for Paris. She hadn't seen that there was a message on the answerphone to say she was going to stay on for a few more days; her brother and his new wife had asked her if she would stay at their house and look after their dog while they were away.

Picking up her coffee mug, she took a sip. Seconds later, the cold coffee and the china mug flew across the office. It made contact with the white board on the far wall. There were lots of arrows and initials which only she understood. The coffee was now running down the board and the wall. She watched as the fluid began to change the words and numbers into an unrecognisable mass of colour and began to cry.

Chapter 70

Steve sat in the wheelchair; a nurse was pushing him along the corridor towards the hydrotherapy pool. He was looking forward to getting into the water.

Moments later, he was floating. The pretty physio was in the pool with him and was supporting his back with minimal effort.

The door opened, and Mari walked in. She blew him a kiss and sat on a wooden bench watching. Mari saw it first. She stood up without saying a word. She had butterflies in her tummy, watching closely to make sure there was no mistake. She held her breath.

"His legs, look at his legs, look!" she shouted.

The physio looked at Steve's legs. They were kicking the water, kicking as if he was going to swim the channel. The two girls looked at Steve. He had the biggest smile ever on his face.

It took a while to get Steve back into his chair. Mari and the physio had to get tough with him, telling him to take things easy. He wanted to try and stand, but the two of them insisted he slow down.

When the three of them got back to the ward, Mari and the nurse stood on either side of the wheelchair with their hands only just supporting him. Steve slowly stood up; he managed to support his own weight and to sit on the side of the bed. After a brief rest, he stood again. With Mari and the nurse by his side, he took his first steps.

Steve could hardly contain his happiness. He was on his feet, one step at a time, concentrating on something the vast majority of us take so much for granted. He was willing his legs to work, and they were. He could feel the cold floor on his bare feet. It was the best thing he had felt for a long time.

Ten minutes later, they did the same thing.

Mari kissed Steve. She gave him strict instructions not to get out of bed until the two of them were with him. As soon as Mari walked out of the ward and the physio disappeared, Steve was sitting back on the side of the bed. He managed the thirty paces to get to the toilet on his own for the first time. He pulled his shorts down and sat on the toilet seat. There were a few magazines next to him, and he looked through them. Good Housekeeping, Woman's Own, two copies of Yachting World, a newspaper, and an old copy of Classic Bike, which he picked up. Despite it being over a year old, he began to read.

Going to the bathroom on your own is one of those things we all take for granted. You lose your dignity when having someone else performing such simple tasks. Steve made the most of his newly regained independence and made himself comfortable.

The ward sister stood at the foot of his bed and looked at him with contempt. At the same time, he could see she was holding a cheeky smile back. She was pleased to see him mobile.

As she walked off, she looked over her shoulder and winked at him. A few minutes later, she returned to his bed.

"You left these in the toilet," she said.

She put the motorcycle magazine and the newspaper on his bed, and, with another wink, she turned and walked off.

Steve winked back and smiled. "The ice queen is melting," he thought, but his smile didn't last long. The newspaper was sitting on his lap, and he saw the front page of the newspaper, the previous days newspaper.

Any doubt about his dreams disappeared immediately. He read the article repeatedly, trying to put a perspective on things. Closing his eyes, he could see Alan's name. He was sure he had the date right. It said 28/09 WATER.

The date on the top of the paper said 29th October. That had meant Alan died on the 28th October, not September. Had he got things wrong? If Alan's date was wrong, could that mean his date could be wrong?

Chapter 71

Sandra sat at one end of the dinner table. At the other end sat her host. She had tried not to laugh at his face. She thought it looked as red as a baboon's arse, but thankfully, she kept her thoughts to herself.

Mr. G was wearing a fluorescent orange Hawaiian shirt, which was too small for him. Only the top two buttons were fastened. His disgustingly huge belly protruded out and pushed into the table. The large plate of oysters sat in front of him. Sandra could see the oyster juice dripping off his chin and then forming a stream between his breasts. He was also smoking one of his fat cigars, the smell of which made Sandra want to choke. She declined the oysters and despite caviar being an option, she sat patiently waiting for her salad.

Mr. G had talked on the phone almost continuously since Sandra had arrived. Now he was spraying a mixture of saliva and oyster juice over the mouthpiece of the onyx handset.

She had come to discuss the fee for the pictures she gave him. He also wanted to know if she wanted to manage his operation in the UK. She needed to find out what was required and, more importantly, how much she was going to get.

She had now decided that one thing was off the menu: her. Despite the potential earnings involved, she was dreading him coming on to her; the thought of him waiting for her to satisfy him repulsed her. "Everyone had a price," she thought. "Everyone except him."

Mr. G loved having a beautiful woman near him; it made him feel even more powerful.

The woman in front of him was wearing a beautiful black dress, and the cut was very low. He liked to see as much cleavage as possible and always insisted his female guests wore the same dress. It was the exact copy of the dress his wife was wearing the night she died twenty years ago; he would never find another woman like her, but he enjoyed the hunt.

One thing he never shared with his dates was the truth about what happened the night his wife died.

He tried to be selective in his memory of the night it happened. He was much younger then and had been drinking heavily. He could still remember the pain he was in. The bullets had hit him exactly where she had wanted them to. He thought she had meant to kill him, but she enjoyed watching him squirm on the bed. It felt and looked as if his guts were pouring out between his legs. It was at this point she changed her mind. Instead of the gun being pointed at his head and putting him out of his misery, she wanted him to suffer.

He knew he deserved it. He wanted to die, but she decided to make herself the ultimate sacrifice.

Wearing the beautiful low cut black dress he had just brought her, he watched her huge fake breasts shake at the same time she pulled the trigger. Two bullets hit him, one in the lower abdomen the other a perfect shot, which hit him between his legs. She pushed the gun up under her chin for the third shot.

He still had no idea what hurt the most, losing his manhood and any chance of sexual pleasure for the rest of his life or tasting and watching his beautiful wife's brains decorate him and their hotel room ceiling.

He now gained great pleasure in making women think he was going to force them to screw him. Very few of his guests ever sat through a whole meal with him, most of them making some excuse or choosing to walk out. The one in front of him now seemed different. "She has balls," he thought. He then chuckled to himself. He also wished he still had balls.

Standing next to Mr G was his minder Conrad; he was also watching Sandra. He hoped more than anyone she would stay. If she did, he would be the one who got to visit her room that evening. He was sure she had been looking at him while his boss was gorging on his food. She only needed to last four more courses. His fingers were crossed behind his back, and he wanted his prize.

During the dessert course, Mr. G spoke to Sandra. He offered her a substantial amount of money. All she needed to do was supply the girls. He now owned a nice hotel on the sea front in Bournemouth, which housed a studio, and he had a crew of people ready for business.

She looked at Mr. G eating his third portion of Tiramisu and then glanced at Conrad, who winked at her. She was hoping he would need to sleep his feast off soon. Thankfully for her, she didn't need to wait long.

Chapter 72

Steve was having difficulty sleeping. The lights were bright. There were nurses trying to comfort a new patient, and his brain would not calm down. Mari came to see him after her shift. She pulled the curtains around his bed and supplied the kind of relaxation therapy which she whispered was not offered on the National Health Service.

It was just after 4 am when Steve began to rewrite his bucket list.

1: Holiday
2: Buy a boat
3:

The list seemed less important now. What he really wanted was to be healthy.

He had money in the bank and someone he wanted to share it with. The thing he really wanted was time. He needed more time and knew that it was the one thing he couldn't buy. All the money in the world couldn't buy the time he needed.

He fell asleep around 5 am, pen still in his hand, and Mari in his heart.

Chapter 73

Sally drove the short distance to Milford through the torrential rain. She was wearing her jogging trousers and an old sweatshirt. She stood outside Billington's apartment. She rang the intercom of number 5, and there was no answer. She knew where there was a key once she got into the lobby. Thankfully, a kind old gentleman carrying three shopping bags saw her; he let her in, and she helped him with his bags into the first apartment. He asked her who she had come to see and when Sally told him he walked over to the sideboard and returned with a note book. He leafed through the pages and confirmed that she had left ten days ago. She got into a Starline taxi at 11:07, and he had not seen her since.

Sally told him she was just going in to water the plants and left the old man looking through his binoculars at something going on in the house opposite.

She walked up the stairs. To the left of number 5's door was a small cupboard where the cleaner kept her supplies, Sally reached behind one of the shelves and found the hidden spare key.

She remembered when she last used it. She surprised Billington on her birthday. She had told Steve she was in London in court, but instead they spent the whole day in bed.

As soon as she opened the door her suspicions were confirmed. The apartment had not been used for a while. The kitchen was spotless, and, upon opening the wardrobe, she saw there were no clothes. Billington's personal items were gone.

As the she opened the door, a man dressed in a tatty looking cheap suit pushed the door towards her. "Who are you?" he asked.

It took seconds for her to notice the old couple standing behind him. Because he was holding a printed sheet with the apartment details on it, she assumed he was an estate agent, and they were looking to buy the apartment

Sally told the man she was checking the place for mail. She gave the key to him and walked out.

Sitting in the car she began to cry; she was now feeling so alone.

Minutes later, she sat in the Needles View café, looking out at the waves crashing against the sea wall. The ice cream tasted amazing.

Sally wondered why her life was spiralling out of control. Sandra had also disappeared off the face of the earth. She could only assume the two of them were together somewhere. She tried to think about why the two of them would do this to her and if it was all about the picture that had been in the magazine, the same picture she found in Steve's pocket when she put his work trousers in the washing machine.

There had to be a connection, and she wanted to find out what the connection was.

She remembered taking the pictures; it started off as a bit of fun. She had been working in the garden office when Sandra paid her a surprise visit. They sat in the garden for some lunch and opened a bottle of wine.

Billington turned up at the cottage a little later and joined them. Two bottles of wine later, Sandra started things off. Sally had gone to the bathroom, and, upon returning to the garden, she saw the two of them kissing.

The photos were their dirty little secret. It wasn't her idea to get other women involved.

Sandra was the one who had the contacts. Her nursing friends loved a bit of excitement.

Sally wondered how many girls had visited the cottage. She could only remember about ten of them but was sure there were more. She still had no idea how one or more had been published; it wasn't something they had agreed on.

Chapter 74

One of the nurses woke Steve. He looked up and he recognised the physio standing by his bed. There were also two more nurses he hadn't seen before, and they were all looking at him.

Steve put his lips together as if to kiss; he made the W sound, followed with a clear "What". Then he said it again: "what". The physio leaned towards him and told him he had been talking in his sleep, clear words.

This was music to his ears; quietly he spoke again. "Where is Mari?" he asked slowly. The physio told him she would get her, and all three of them walked towards the nurse station.

A few minutes later, Mari was sitting by his side, and there were tears of joy in her eyes as they quietly talked.

Slowly but surely, Mari was getting her man back. Steve put his head back on the pillow and shut his eyes. Within seconds, he was asleep.

Mari saw the doctor who was responsible for Steve and went over to give him the good news. When he saw her, he asked her to meet him in his office in ten minutes. She smiled and headed towards the canteen.

Twenty minutes later and apologising profusely, he walked into the waiting area next to his office. He opened the door and ushered Mari in. She sat in a chair in front of his beautiful antique desk.

Mari listened to the doctor's every word. She could understand the medical terms he was referring to and although she was smiling, she knew that things could be different. The doctors were now thinking that Steve may have had a seizure, and they wanted to do more tests. If they couldn't find anything, then Steve could be released in a couple of days. He had

made great progress, and, as long as he could walk to the bathroom and back unaided, they felt he could manage at home.

Mari felt more positive now than in the last week, and she returned to the ward to give Steve the news.

Chapter 75

Sandra was sitting in the back of the Bentley that picked her up from the airport. It was nice to be back in the UK. As much as she loved the hot weather, she missed her home comforts, especially her coffee.

She was living the millionaire lifestyle, and, as the car got closer to home, she prayed she would see someone she recognised. She didn't.

The driver, who was wearing the full chauffeur uniform, pulled up right outside her complex. He got out of the car and opened the door for her. After another quick look around, her disappointment was confirmed; there was no one watching. Despite the man not saying a word to her during the whole journey, she couldn't resist kissing him on the cheek as he took her small case out of the car boot. For a moment, she thought he smiled, but she could have been wrong.

As she pushed the door open, she could tell something was wrong. She could see from the front door that someone had been in. She shouted, "I'm home", just in case there was someone still inside. She stood with her mouth open, listening for a moment. She was aware of the smell first; something had been burned. For a moment, she wondered if she had left her hair tongs on when she left, but she then noticed the broken smoke detector above her. She walked along the hallway to the kitchen door on her left. She pushed the door open with her foot but pushed it too hard. The door handle on the back of the door hit the wall hard with a metallic thud.

Slowly walking in, her heart sunk. The room had been completely trashed; three of the cupboard doors were ripped off, and the contents of every cupboard left on the wood floor.

Looking around at the mess, there didn't seem to be a packet or box that had not been opened. She noticed the two empty packets of her beloved coffee, both empty, and the contents, she could see, had been thrown around the room. This especially made her grit her teeth. Slowly, she retraced her steps back into the hallway and walked gingerly into the lounge. It was the same story here. The few ornaments she owned had been thrown against the wall. One of them, a large Poole Pottery glass bowl, had also been thrown against the small tropical fish tank. The dead fish lay on the white carpet along with the white stones from the tank and fragments of orange glass. Being careful not to touch too much, she felt the carpet which was still slightly damp. Sandra guessed this must have happened a few days ago otherwise the carpet would have been much wetter.

Standing on the spot, Sandra looked around the room. Nothing had been untouched; the glass dining table had been shattered, and the laminated pieces were left in a big pile where they fell. Her beautiful white sofa had been cut with a knife or blade, the foam and contents of the cushions scattered around the room.

The bedroom was in a similar state; even the mattress had been cut open. Every drawer had been taken out and their contents again scattered on the floor. Stepping over her now ripped clothes, she opened the walk in wardrobe. She knew this would tip her over the edge. Upon opening the door, her stomach churned. She discovered where the burning smell came from. Her underwear, the most precious of all her belongings, lay on the floor in a charred pile. Her first thoughts were, "How? How could have anyone done this? The whole house was alarmed."

She looked up and could see the other smoke detector; it was open, and the battery removed. Looking over her shoulder and up to the bedroom ceiling, the other detector was missing. The bathroom was the last room she entered. The wall-sized mirror was shattered into a million pieces on the polished marble, and a similar smell drew her eyes into the bath. Her beautiful standalone ceramic white bath contained what was now the charred remains of her perfumes, her makeup, and the most expensive lotions she could have found. There was still the smell of lighter fuel in the air. Sitting on the toilet seat, she was too shocked to cry; her head was spinning, and she had never felt so sick in her life.

There were so many questions in her mind. Who? Why? How? Trying to keep calm, she picked up her phone and began to look through her phone book. She was looking for someone who would clean up the mess and also looking at the names of people she suspected would have done this to her. She got to the end of her directory, knowing there was only one person who would have done this. Sandra looked around again, and she couldn't help thinking that a lot of time and effort had been put into creating the horror she was looking at.

Standing up and reaching into the bath to retrieve a bottle of Chanel perfume, she cleaned the bottle on a towel before noticing it was empty.

A few minutes later, she walked towards her car in the underground car park. She noticed the broken windscreen first. Upon getting closer, she could see the scratches; every panel was damaged.

The car opened with a loud plip, and Sandra put the key under the driver's seat, shut the door, and walked up the ramp into the street just as a taxi approached. On the way into town, she phoned her garage, they agreed to pick the car up in two day's time.

Chapter 76

Steve had his bag packed. Having walked to the bathroom from his bed three times and showing no evidence of epilepsy, the doctor had kept his word and agreed to let him go home. Mari would finish her shift at 3 pm, and a taxi had been booked to take them the short journey to her apartment. She had not said anything to Steve, but they were also going to look at a house that had just come on the rental market. There were two bedrooms and a small garden. It was only down the road from where she currently lived, and she hoped that this would be a fresh start for them both.

Steve lay on the hospital bed and closed his eyes. He was imagining the two of them on a boat, a big yacht. He could feel the heat on his face. He could see the sun and the deep blue sky. The sky was turning from blue to white, very white. He looked down; the yacht had gone, and he was now on his own. Looking around, he knew where he was. He had lost control of his thoughts. It felt as if there was someone forcing his head as he tried to resist looking down, but his eyes were wide open.

Trying to close them and make the dream end, he felt as if he were being held in a straightjacket suspended from the sky, the brilliant white sky. The whiteness almost burning his eyes, he had no choice now. The familiar white table was in front of him, and the book was on it. It wasn't there a second ago; just like the previous times, the cover of the white book opened, and the pages moved from right to left. Steve tried to focus his eyes, but the light in the room was so bright. This felt different; his eyes were hurting, and he could feel them watering. He tried to focus again on the pages and could see columns, but this time they were on every page. He tried harder to focus on the names. As he thought he recognised a name, the page turned and then another. He tried even harder, willing himself to move closer. He could feel his body straining. The book sat flat on the desk in front of him in the same position, its pages still turning. He saw letters he recognised:

PA.

He was guessing now; was this Sally's mother?

He felt so helpless as the page turned before he could focus on the remainder of the letters, but, at last, the pages seemed to be slowing down. He saw

"Robert" followed by "Alan" and "Dean".

Steve guessed what was coming next.

The pages stopped.

In front of him, as clear as it could be,

Steve stared at what he saw.

"You, 01/11, Shot".

Staring at the page, Steve felt confused. This was wrong, the wrong date. He was willing the page to turn again, but there was nothing, no movement, no air. He couldn't breathe. His chest was pushing into him, his throat tightening, and he could feel his last breath leave him.

His eyes were transfixed on the page.

01/11. "No, that's wrong!" he tried to scream, but no sound left him.

His eyes felt as if they were going to explode, and the veins in his head were pulsating. The pressure on his body was now so intense, a pain like he had never experienced. The brilliant white light began to dim. All he could do was look at the page one last time. In the last moments of his life, he could see the date, though it was getting dimmer.

The number "one" faded as did the other "one", followed by the "/". Then, as the light had almost gone, the date changed again.

He saw 12/11.

He coughed. Air, air at last. Desperately trying to get as much oxygen into his lungs, he fought against the intense pain and heard the words,

"Give him another shot."

The noise was like no other.

It sounded like someone dropping a watermelon off a building but a thousand times louder. He could taste the air, pure air. Gasping every molecule into his lungs as if it were his last but feeling as if it was his first, he could feel the mask over his face and now hear voices. There was someone crying, and a man calling his name. There was a flash in one eye then the other as Steve tried to open his eyes. They were sore, his throat hurt, and he was shivering; his whole body ached.

Trying to focus on what was going on, the first thing he understood was a man's voice.

"Welcome back old boy," followed by the most beautiful sound in the world. He heard Mari, crying but pleading,

"I love you so much, please don't leave me."

It took a while to understand what had happened, but again he thought

"This is not the day to die."

Mari stood beside the doctor and her fellow nurses. They were working hard to save their patient. If not for a passing visitor who noticed his blue face, Steve would have died.

Two hours earlier, she was making plans for the future, now she was watching and hoping with all her heart that the man she was in love with would live.

It took two attempts with the defibrillator to get Steve breathing. The first 200 volts didn't work so the doctor increased it to 320 volts. That worked and the heart monitor was showing a healthy rhythm; they all stood back as Steve opened his eyes. He could see his audience and realised his latest dream almost cost him his life.

It was over an hour later the oxygen mask was removed. The odd thing was that Steve felt fine; there were sticky pads all over his chest, and he was still wired up to the monitor. Mari was looking with interest at the notes and the results of one of the blood tests that had been done. The doctor who administered the shocks was also back to check on his patient.

Steve had his eyes closed. He could see the book, and he watched the date change again. He could see the date, transfixed in his mind. "It must be wrong, it's got to be wrong", he thought.

He was trying to work out what to tell Mari; he could picture the two of them sitting in his favourite Thai restaurant.

"I do love you Mari, and I'm going to die in 11 days."

Now convinced that the revised date was his day to die, he had to think about what he should do. He had less than two weeks to live. He wanted to make every second count. The first thing he needed to do was to get out of hospital. That might be easier said than done. He opened his eyes and looked at the people standing around him.

"All I need to do is convince this lot I need out of here," he thought.

Chapter 77

Having phoned a friend who owned a domestic cleaning company, Sandra checked herself into the Bournemouth Hilton. She knew the hotel well, and, along with knowing some of the staff well, she felt safe there.

With her only salvageable possessions in a travel case, she opened the hotel room and remembered the last time she had been there; she could have made a fortune by going to the papers with the pictures she took that night but had kept them just in case she needed to call in a favour.

Those pictures and many more she knew were kept in one of four safety deposit boxes she rented in the basement of the hotel.

Walking out on the balcony, she looked over the Bournemouth skyline; the sun was low in the sky, and the view reminded her how much she loved the town.

"You can take the girl out of Bournemouth . . .

but you can never take Bournemouth out of the girl," she said, while holding up an ice-cold gin and tonic as if toasting the town.

The cool air made her shudder. Walking back into the room and sliding the large glass door closed behind her, she walked into the bathroom.

A while later, she stood naked in front of the full-length mirror, admiring her figure. She cupped her breasts in her hands, still undecided if her boobs would look better bigger or smaller. She only had a week to decide.

There was a knock at the door.

"Room service."

The uniformed young man stood at the door; he knocked the door again and waited for a reply.

The door opened, and he nearly dropped the tray balancing in his right palm. Standing in front of him was a beautiful woman. She was wearing red silk panties and a naughty smile. She took the tray, blew him a kiss, and shut the door.

As she walked over to the bed, she smiled and hoped that her requirements from room service would exceed her expectations during her stay.

Sandra needed to decide on her next move. She was due back at the clinic in the morning but desperately needed to go shopping for clothes and cosmetics. She rang room service who assured her a taxi would be outside the hotel in one hour. It was.

Chapter 78

Sally had been stuck in the traffic for over an hour. The police had walked towards them, talking to every driver in turn and were approaching her car. She wound the window down and listened to her instructions.

Sally's thoughts were with the people up ahead; she could hear the rotors of the helicopter above her and knew this was always an indication of a serious accident. Unfortunately, when this part of the Wessex Way became blocked, it was impossible to pass any incident until it had been cleared.

Another 30 minutes passed. It was starting to get dark. In front of her was a sea of blue flashing lights that were giving her a headache.

She could see the police erecting a blue tent. This was commonly used to hide something from prying eyes.

Chapter 79

There was no pain. The intravenous line in her right wrist was seeing to that. It was cold, and the blankets and sea of silver foil failed to warm her. There were so many blue lights flashing it looked as if her rescuers were moving in a strobe like robots. The air she was breathing was pure oxygen. It tasted sweet. The temptation to close her eyes was huge, but the girl in the high viz vest who was talking to her and holding a pad to the top of her head was urging her not to close them.

With the knowledge she had gained in her profession, she understood the importance of keeping calm, still, and awake. She also knew that she was in a bad way but not as bad as the driver. She guessed there was nothing anyone could do about him as they were concentrating on her. His limp body still sat in the driver's seat in front of her. She tried not to look at the amount of crimson blood soaking into the carpet by her feet again. She hoped it wasn't hers. Sandra was already doing a self-assessment on her own injuries. Her obvious concern was her face. She could only see clearly out of one eye and hoped this was due to the blood that had begun to dry. She could feel her teeth with her tongue. This was good as they had cost her thousands of pounds.

She felt very tired but knew she needed to stay awake. She wanted to be a model patient.

She wondered how much longer she was going to be kept in the cold. She was more aware of it now and guessed that the loss of blood may have something to do with it.

The paramedic was talking to her, but she couldn't hear her. Then she realised she couldn't hear anything; despite the chaos in front of her failing eyes, it was silent.

Sandra felt as if she had managed to slow the world down, but her thoughts were as clear as they could be.

She thought about her mother; she owed the woman so much and wished she could apologise to her. She knew Claire was ill but had chosen to ignore her existence.

Sandra also reflected on her biggest secret about the woman who never even knew she had a sister, the woman she loved, the woman she despised, the woman who took her father away from her.

Tears ran down her cheeks and everything was becoming blurred. Her eyes began to close.

The paramedic, who Sandra remembered introducing herself as Sam, was now covering her with a black sheet. A moment later, a machine was working behind the seat. She knew enough to understand that she had to be removed from the car, and she was going to be put onto one or two backboards to be taken out where the roof had been. The noise she heard was the hydraulic cutter. This was making the exit route bigger by cutting the roof away from the car.

Sam was doing all she could to keep her patient alive. Constantly reassuring her that they were helping and doing their best to get her out as soon as possible. She knew her patient had lost lots of blood. Her main objective was to try to keep her patient alive. She could see that there was an area as big as her fist of Sandra's skull missing. Nothing much surprised Sam, but she had no idea how the woman in front of her was still conscious. Sam's partner was pushing as much fluid into Sandra's arm as he could.

The helicopter was two hundred yards away on the opposite carriageway and waiting to take her to Southampton Hospital. Sandra wasn't aware of this. She was also unaware of the two pieces of scaffolding tube.

One had hit the driver in the throat, it was still there but half a meter of it was poking out of the perfect round hole in the car roof.

The second pole had gone right through the car and was laying in the road behind them.

The emergency doctor knelt where the front passenger seat had been. He was flashing his torch into Sandra's eyes, which were slowly closing.

The emergency services worked as fast as they could, and, seven minutes later, Helmed One Zero took off on course for South-ampton General Hospital.

It took another hour to release the traffic. Every car for a four-mile stretch of the Wessex Way had to turn around and drive the wrong way down the dual carriageway until they could exit. The police did the best they could, and, fortunately, the majority of drivers understood.

Steve slept until 5 am. He threw the sheets off the bed and walked towards the bathroom. Before he had a chance to object, a wheelchair was thrust beneath him. The night nurse was not very happy and insisted on waiting outside the door in case she was needed.

After being helped back into bed, he sat and began to work out his escape. He needed to get Mari to help him, because, without her, the next 11 days would be unbearable.

Chapter 80

Sitting in her small apartment, Mari was watching the local news. She could see one car on its roof, and there was another hidden by the blue sheets. She had been working that afternoon, and, although she was on her ward, there was talk of a fatal car accident.

In the canteen that afternoon, she also heard a fellow nurse talking about the incident. Apparently, a taxi ran into the back of a stationary truck carrying scaffolding tubes, and then another vehicle hit the back of the taxi, which caused it to overturn.

There had been one or two fatalities, but the three people in the overturned car got away with minor injuries.

Mari thought for a moment of all the people affected. She knew too well the impact of a bad accident; she had lost two brothers in their late teens when their car went off the road in Corfu.

Her mother never got over the accident and died, Mari thought of a broken heart less than a year later. Her father, who was still alive, decided that drink was the correct way to numb the pain of grief.

This prompted her to call him. There was a two-hour time difference, and she knew he would be at home. The next forty minutes were spent telling him about the man she was in love with who wanted to see the island. She also asked after her uncle Costas, because they were hoping he could help her rent a boat for a day or two while they were visiting.

Russell D Whitney

As she sat in bed, she closed her eyes and began to pray. Religion was important, and she believed her life was at last changing for the better. Hoping her beloved man would be home very soon, she fell asleep.

Chapter 81

The new patient in the Intensive Care Unit at Southampton General Hospital lay in one of the twenty-five beds on the ward. Usually, there is one nurse per patient, but for severe cases, there could be two dedicated nurses. This patient needed two.

Now in a medically induced coma, she was on a mechanical ventilator. Tests and scans had already been done, and, at this stage, it was a waiting game. When the air ambulance landed, Sandra was taken straight to the operating theatre. It took five hours to stabilise her. The list of injuries was horrific.

She had one broken femur, a shattered pelvis, nine broken ribs, two punctured lungs caused by the ribs, and one of her breast implants had been ruptured by the car seat belt and had to be removed.

The biggest concern was the trauma to her head, caused by a piece of steel or aluminium tubing which had passed through the car at the point of impact. The surgeon who operated on her skull had tried to save the piece of dislodged bone, but unfortunately. A skin graft had to be taken from other areas of the skull.

It was unsure how much damage had been caused to the brain at this stage. Surprisingly the brain scan showed very little damage, but when the brain has a bleed and open trauma, it may well have been affected.

The first one or two days were critical in cases like this. The patient was reported to be conscious for a time during the extraction from the car, which the surgeon found hard to believe.

It was one of the ICU nurses that recognised the patient. Her identity was confirmed by the personal items in her bag, which were recovered at the scene of the accident, and Sandra's medical records were accessed immediately.

There was no next of kin on any of the notes, and the police were getting her phone unlocked to see if they could find the number of someone they could contact.

Sandra owned two phones: one for business and one for personal use.

The phone the police were unlocking was the business phone. She only took incoming calls on it with one exception: a number she had called twelve times the previous day.

Her other phone was stuck to the carpet by dried blood under the driver's seat of the Mercedes, which was waiting for the accident investigation team near Poole.

The police had looked at footage from one of the cameras that operated at the junction where the accident happened; the scaffolding truck clearly braked suddenly and smoke could be seen from the rear tyres.

One officer remarked that it looked as if the driver of the truck decided at the last moment not to proceed with the left turn when the lights turned from amber to red.

The taxi following the truck didn't seem to slow down at all. One of the officers zoomed in and could see the taxi hitting the truck. There was no indication from the brake lights on the taxi of any attempt to slow down. There were scaffolding pipes overhanging the rear of the truck and the officers could see the taxi windscreen was touching the back of the truck and all four wheels were almost off the ground as if it was being suspended.

The vehicle behind the taxi also failed to stop. Frame by frame the officers watched the car suddenly swerve, but it caught the corner of the taxi. It must have been quite an impact as the car flipped onto its side and then its roof. After that, it slid along the road out of camera shot.

There had to be a formal examination of the car, but it looked clear as to what happened to the vehicles. The investigation would look at why the taxi didn't stop, the driver could have been distracted or fallen asleep or had a heart attack. That hopefully would be resolved by a post-mortem of the driver's body.

Chapter 82

Sally sat on the huge sofa, watching TV. The weather was supposed to get better later in the day, and she was hoping to get on the famous steam train for afternoon tea.

The cottage she had rented was in the middle of the town. From where she was sitting, she could see out of the window the beautiful multi coloured quaint cottages and shops along the high street, which, in any weather, looked so typically Kentish.

It was Sally's parents who introduced her to Tenterden. They had stayed in the same cottage when she had been a child, and the town reminded her so much of her privileged upbringing. She was so happy to find the house still available to rent, and she needed the rest. She needed to decide what to do with her life, and, more importantly, she needed to decide who she wanted in her life.

Chapter 83

Steve sat on the edge of his bed. He had been dressed since 7:30 and was expecting to see the doctor at 9:30. He looked at his watch again; only three minutes had passed since he last looked.

The ward sister had already told him it was unlikely he would be going home yet, but Steve couldn't afford to be in hospital.

He had decided on a plan and was going to insist his recovery would be better at home. After all, he would be in the best of hands.

Secondly, he needed to get Mari to agree they needed a holiday; that would also aid any recovery.

Thirdly, Mari had no reason to know about the dream; if he was going to die-which Steve was now a hundred percent sure he was-he wanted to go in style.

He had already ruled out doing a Thelma and Louise and driving off the clifftop in Barton-on-Sea. He thought about the two of them going to Vegas, but he knew Mari would object.

One thing he knew for sure was that a trip to Corfu would be easy to arrange. He also knew Mari had a cousin who could possibly lend or, if he had to, buy a boat from.

Steve still wondered how he would be shot but found irony in a book Mari gave him to read about Corfu. Shooting is one of the biggest pastimes for men during the winter on the island.

Another glance at his watch confirmed there was still over an hour to wait, so he decided to go and find the shop. He was craving some chocolate and a San Miguel, but he settled for the chocolate.

Sally rang her personal bank manager; she was worried because she was ten minutes late. Thankfully, he was able to talk and was pleased to hear from her. He urged her to move the payment that was transferred the previous evening. He knew if she had her finances investigated, he could be in serious trouble. He had known her all her life, and he was one of the only people Sally could trust. She asked him to deal with it as he always did.

Sally was getting more worried about the money in her accounts and had even asked for the payments to stop. She knew she would also be in serious trouble if the truth was discovered.

Steve read the front pages of the day's papers and looked at the headline on the Echo: another bad accident. Opting for the latest Classic Car Magazine and two bars of their cheapest chocolate, he returned to the ward.

Half an hour later, the ward sister told Steve that the doctor he needed to see had been called to another hospital, and he would hopefully be back at 4 pm. Feeling extremely frustrated, Steve sat back on his bed and opened the second bar of chocolate.

At five to ten, Mari walked onto the ward. On hearing of the delay, she looked as disappointed as Steve felt. She was not due to begin her shift until 1 pm so the two of them walked into the garden. The rain had stopped, and they sat under a huge umbrella, watching the birds and discussing which restaurant to go to that evening.

Mari got upset when Steve began to talk about wanting to discharge himself and insisted on him waiting until he had been cleared by the doctor. She didn't tell him that it was unlikely he would be released for at least another day, possibly two.

At 4 pm, Steve stood at the nurse station and was told that the doctor was on his way. This also happened at 5 and at 5:30 pm.

The big station style clock on the wall above the ward entrance showed 6 pm, and Steve's heart rate was through the roof. He was agitated and extremely frustrated. Just as he had considered walking out and not returning, the doctor walked in. He had a big smile on his face and walked over to the ward sister and placed his arm around her. Steve noticed the look on her face was that of distaste.

It took another twenty-seven minutes before the man stood in front of Steve, who was sitting on the side of his bed with his shoes on and his small case packed on the floor ready to go.

Why the doctor smiled at Steve so much puzzled him. After another blood pressure test was taken, the doctor announced that the reading was far too high for his patient to go anywhere.

Steve rarely swore; on this occasion, his voice could be heard at the end of the ward.

Despite explaining that he should have been seen eight hours ago and insisting this was the reason for his blood pressure being high, the doctor stuck by his decision.

Steve watched him walk out of the ward and sat down in the chair next to his bed.

He was still there when Mari appeared. She knew what he had been told and was also disappointed, but she did have some good news. She had been granted two weeks annual leave as of two days' time. This was the best news he could have hoped for and began to rewrite his plan.

185

Chapter 84

After the previous day's disappointment, Steve decided on a different approach to the morning. He ate breakfast in bed and took longer than usual in the shower and sitting on the toilet. At two minutes to ten, he casually walked down the ward, and, to his utter surprise, the doctor and Mari were waiting for him.

Steve could tell by looking at Mari that he may stand a chance of escaping.

The doctor calmly explained that if his blood pressure was ok, he could be discharged.

The next three minutes felt like three hours.

On releasing the tourniquet, the doctor looked at him and said three words he was literally dying to hear.

"Off you go," was all he said, and, without a further word, the man turned his back on his patient and walked off.

It was Mari who sat with him, going through the rules. This included what pills to take, food to eat, and how much water to drink. She had also had her leave extended so she could look after him straight away.

Thirty minutes later, the taxi pulled up outside the apartment. Mari had already rescheduled the viewing on the house she had seen, but she wanted Steve to have a rest first.

It was the first disagreement they had. Mari ended up going to see the house on her own, and she didn't understand Steve's reluctance to even consider a bigger place.

The house was perfect; she could picture the two of them spending lots of time in the small garden, and it was in lovely condition. It also backed on to a park. Still feeling there was some hope, she walked into her apartment. Steve was missing, and there was a message written on the chalkboard attached to the fridge.

"Gone Shopping P.S. Love You XX."

Three long hours passed, and Mari was contemplating calling the police when the front door opened.

She threw her arms around him and apologised for wanting to move home. He was equally as sorry and agreed that they would talk about moving when they got home.

Mari looked confused for a moment, but, upon looking at the receipt being handed to her, she understood what he meant.

She read the piece of paper in her hand and tears of joy filled her eyes. Steve had the biggest smile on his face she had ever seen. The reality of her returning home to Corfu was sinking in.

They were going on what she assumed was the trip of a lifetime.

If only she knew it was to be the trip to end a lifetime.

In the morning, the two of them were to catch the train to London then another to Gatwick. They were to fly to Bari in Italy, and, the following day, they were due to catch an overnight ferry to Corfu.

An hour later, the two of them were drinking hot chocolate while sitting in the little café on the clifftop in Southbourne. For a November day, the sun was out and the wind light. The view east over to the Isle of Wight and then west to Bournemouth was one of Steve's favourites.

That evening, the two of them packed their bags. It was nearly midnight before the two of them got into bed. Mari fell asleep in seconds; her heavy breathing made Steve smile. He had missed her so much. He closed his eyes, but there was no way he was going to sleep. His mind was working overtime.

Still questioning the dates in his dreams, he was going through them again. He had so many questions, but now there was no one he could talk to about them.

Yet again, he was keeping his thoughts to himself. He wondered if he could tell Mari what was going on in his mind. But would she believe him? Would she understand?

Chapter 85

Mari woke at 5:30 and went to put her arms around Steve. She called out to him the moment she realised he wasn't in bed with her, and, to her relief, he put his head round the door and blew her a kiss.

At 11:03, the Gatwick Express train pulled into the station, having already booked in. It didn't take long before the two of them were through departures and looking around the duty-free shops. Mari insisted she brought herself some perfume and wanted to try on some dresses so Steve wandered over to the Omega watch shop. He had always wanted an expensive watch and looked in the window. He couldn't see the prices so walked in where he was greeted by a pretty assistant. Her name badge read Leva.

A few minutes later, he was looking at the most beautiful timepiece. It looked simple but sophisticated with a black leather strap, silver body and face, with a ceramic bezel.

Steve listened to the enthusiasm that the girl had for the watch. He didn't understand the technical details but assumed, at just over 8000 euro, it must be good.

Moments later, he was walking out of the shop. The Omega Speedmaster was in its box, which was laying inside a carrier bag next to the three motorcycle magazines and a bottle of water.

189

Russell D Whitney

Mari came bounding over to him, insisting he looked at the new skirt she brought. Feeling guilty about how much he spent, he decided not to say anything about his purchase.

The flight took just under three hours. Steve found himself looking at the inflight magazine, and his eyes lit up when he found an article all about watches. He read it with interest and understood what Leva had told him earlier. He decided not to wear it until later that evening.

He had booked one of the most exclusive hotels in one of the most amazing places in Italy and was almost having to bite his lip as not to tell Mari where they were going.

The Plazzo Gattini Luxury Hotel was the best hotel the travel agent could recommend. It is positioned within the UNESCO world heritage site of Matera. The hotel was built in traditional stone and offered superb facilities.

Steve had wanted to visit Matera since he was a boy. He remembered seeing the city on television and read up on the area as part of a school project. Ever since then, he had dreamed of going, and they were going to stay somewhere so beautiful. He was so excited and knew he was making memories; unfortunately, his memories wouldn't last long.

In the back of the taxi, the two of them hung on for dear life. The driver wanted to overtake anything that was in front of him, and whilst Steve wanted to tell the driver to slow down, Mari seemed to be enjoying the ride. He kept quiet and held on with white knuckles to the seatbelt.

The front of the hotel looked exactly like the pictures in the brochure; softly lit lights shining in the arches made them look as if they had been carved out of gold, the majestic stonewalls and arches are described as:

"The most striking sculpture of stone ever made in human history."

They were met by the white gloved porter who looked magnificent in his uniform. He guided them into the reception area where they were met by the hotel manager and two receptionists. There was a tranquil atmosphere.

Steve and Mari stood in the reception just looking around them. Words alone could not do such a wonderful place justice. They were immersed in an experience that continued to give. The arches continued as they were ushered to a heavy dark wooden door, which was opened silently to reveal the most stunning room either of them had ever seen.

The walls were again in traditional stone. There were three small cut-outs in the wall above the immaculate super king-sized bed, and each of them was lit by a blue shimmering light. At the end of the room, another lit stone arch, which led to the bathroom. Mari walked in first. Steve could see the tears of joy as she looked at the sunken stone bath, and the walk-in shower was bigger than her lounge at home. Neither of them had ever experienced such luxury.

There was one more archway in the main room. The bellboy opened the two small doors and handed them both a glass of champagne before leaving. Walking on to the balcony, the city was revealed in its evening splendour.

The view was priceless. Matera seemed to be waiting for them to appreciate it. Hundreds of small buildings stretched as far as the eye could see. Many seemed to have a light twinkling in the windows, but the darkness of the evening still hung motionless and complimented the view.

The light from the moon lit the whole city, it looked as if there had been a shower of golden drops, the air was cold but the view in front of the couple's eyes warmed them as they took in the most wonderful sight.

Dinner was also better than either of them could have wished for. The menu was confusing for Steve, but the waiter, who had attended university in Brighton, spoke perfect English, and he translated the options and helped to choose the correct wines with the seven courses.

Steve was wearing his new Omega watch and couldn't help looking at it every few minutes. Mari asked him if he was in a hurry or if he had to go elsewhere so he confessed about the purchase. Thankfully, she didn't ask how much it cost.

One of the wonderful things about Matera are best seen from a different perspective.

On walking through the modern part of the city, if you are traveling in the right direction, you get to an iron railing.

Looking beyond the railing, the old city looks as if it has been built in a quarry, and from this vantage point, you can almost see the whole city.

The chilly wind made it uncomfortable to stand for too long. Steve and Mari had the whole of the next day to explore the breath-taking city. The ferries to Corfu didn't leave Bari port until 9 pm the following evening.

Steve sat on the bed, sipping his glass of champagne and heard Mari turn on the shower. He walked over to the open bathroom door and watched as she washed her hair. The shampoo covered her olive skin, and the clean water washed the white foam off, revealing her toned body. She pumped some lotion out of the container on the wall, and, using her hands, she rubbed it into her shoulders. Stepping away from the perfect circle of water, she continued to rub the lotion over her body. Her back was to the door, and she didn't notice Steve watching. It was making him lightheaded; he could feel blood draining from his brain to supply another part of his body.

Mari ran her hands over her small firm breasts and pinched her nipples. It made her flinch. The feeling was heavenly. She closed her eyes as her hands slid over her stomach to the top of her thighs.

She opened her eyes and turned so she could back into the cascading water. As she did so, she saw Steve standing in the doorway and smiled at him.

Steve didn't move. He watched as Mari ran her hands all over her body rinsing the lotion off. She smiled at him again as he stood naked in front of her. She teased him a while longer, making him wait to be invited to join her. He didn't wait long.

Mari turned her back as Steve stepped into the spray; he pushed his body against hers and placed his hands on her hips, pulling her closer to him. Kissing her neck made her shudder. She pushed the cheeks of her bottom into him. She reached round, took his right hand, and placed it between her legs. He knew what she wanted, and he was happy to oblige.

They dried each other with the soft white towels, and Mari took his hand and led him naked through the bedroom to the arch. She opened the door and walked out on to the cold dark balcony. She looked over her shoulder at him, leaving him in no doubt about exactly what she wanted.

Steve hadn't expected to be making love on the balcony in full view of anyone who had wanted to watch. He smiled to himself and was grateful for the cool breeze and hoped all the sensible people of Matera were in their nice warm houses.

Chapter 86

05/11 – 7 DAYS TO DIE DAY

Breakfast was delivered to the room at 8 am, a continental tray of croissants, pastries, fresh fruit, and yoghurt, along with the finest Italian coffee and fresh juices. Steve was keen to explore the city, especially as the weather looked so well. No rain was due, and the low sun was already warming the air.

Every little square revealed more houses, little streets, and numerous restaurants. The two of them lasted until 11 am before they sat for a coffee and the best ice cream they had ever tasted.

Dinner that evening had been arranged back at the hotel, and, after a quick shower, the two of them climbed into a taxi for an hour ride. Steve was relieved to see it wasn't the same driver who picked them up at the airport, but ten minutes later, he was wishing it had been.

Even Mari looked worried as the taxi weaved its way through small villages. They weren't sure if the driver had a death wish or if he was late for his dinner. A journey that should have taken an hour took forty minutes. Even the driver looked relieved when he parked the car at the departures entrance of the port.

It took a while to get checked in, and, thankfully, Steve had booked a cabin. The wind had picked up, and they were informed at the check-in desk that the crossing to Corfu Port may be a little rough. On the plus side, the estimated time of arrival was still 5 am.

Mari began to feel ill around 10.30 pm. She had been yawning, which, alongside being tired, was a possible sign of seasickness.

Steve left Mari bent over the toilet bowl and went out to get some fresh air. The waves were breaching the bow of the ship, and, within seconds, a plume of water headed towards him. Despite ducking below the solid rail in front of him, it soaked him. Feeling like a child avoiding the waves, he stuck his head over the rail one more time and caught a face full of spray. It was freezing and instantly made Steve regret leaving the cabin. He was drenched.

The smell of vomit in the cabin also made Steve feel ill. Mari now had nothing left inside her to bring up. She was lying on the bed, holding a plastic mug should she need it.

It was a tortuous three more hours until the ship became more stable. It was then that the two of them fell asleep. They both managed just under three hours before the tannoy announced they were nearing their destination.

Chapter 87

The two of them stood on the deck of the ship. The sea was dead flat as they watched the Port of Corfu come into sight.

Seeing the early 15th Century Old Fortress lit up always made Mari feel so proud to be a Corfiot. In 1798, some male members of her family were involved in The Siege of Corfu. She was very proud of her heritage, and she vowed to show Steve the graves where some of her relatives had been buried.

As the ferry got closer to the dock, Mari's thoughts were with her two brothers and her mother. She missed them so much. She cuddled her man and hoped she would not have to deal with losing someone close to her again.

The ferry docked at 5:45, and the two of them walked off, dragging their cases. Steve's fingers were crossed as tight as possible while they waited for a taxi.

"The driver's here couldn't be any worse than the Italians," he said. Mari looked at him with a smile, the kind of smile that implied she knew the answer but was keeping it to herself.

The driver took nearly 30 minutes to get to the Village of Benitses. It was only a 10km journey. Only the near side headlight was working on the old taxi, and the sun had yet to appear. Steve was sure the driver was using brail to navigate the unlit and unmarked main highway.

Mari had a cousin who owned a restaurant in Benitses Village and hoped he would cook them something to eat. She was also very keen to get out of the car.

Chapter 88

Sally sat up in bed; it was only 4:50 am. She was due to return to the cottage later in the day, but she was distracted by the phone call she received the previous evening.

The call was from Hampshire Police.

She thought her heart was trying to escape through her mouth, and her immediate thought was to defend herself. She soon found out that was not necessary.

The detective asked Sally if she knew Sandra. When she answered in the affirmative, the detective began questioning the nature of their relationship.

She was told that Sandra had been in a road traffic accident, and they were trying to reach any close relations. The reason for the call was that Sally's number was the only one on her phone. Sally knew why.

She told the detective they were just friends, and she had no idea if any of Sandra's relations were still alive.

She decided not to say that Sandra's mother had disowned her because of her choice of lifestyle.

The detective asked if Sally would meet him at Southampton Hospital as soon as possible.

Except for saying Sandra was in the Critical Care Unit, he wouldn't give her any more information over the phone.

She agreed to meet him at 4 pm.

Chapter 89

The huge orange ball peeked below the bulbous white clouds that hung in the air over the mainland mountains, sending waves of sun onto the sea. The whole sky looked alight. The slight breeze was making the steel rigging of the yachts in the harbour hit the masts with a metallic clang.

Men stood in their small fishing boats, throwing nets into the water and becoming silhouetted against the light. Even in November, the temperature was comfortable.

The sea lapped at the rocks a metre below them while a stray cat sat watching and hoping for some scraps.

This was Steve's first sunrise in Corfu, and he was in awe of the view in front of him. A young woman in the tightest of running shorts passed the two of them, and Steve couldn't help watch as she ran out of sight. He then looked at Mari who was standing in front of him; her arms were crossed, and she rolled her eyes at him.

With a sheepish grin, he stood up and put his arms around her.

From the other side of the road, Mari's cousin was calling; he had opened his taverna early just for them, and there was a feast laying on the table.

Mari and Steve sat at the table with Dimitris, his wife, and their four small children. The freshly baked bread was still warm. The smell was making their mouths water, and the sight of fresh fish, olives, figs, fruit, and juices were welcome.

Dimitris then told Mari her father was on his way. He travelled everywhere on his old vespa scooter and was due in the next half hour.

Steve had his plate filled in seconds. Mari, although starving hungry, was now too excited to eat. She walked up to the main road to meet her father. Twenty minutes later, the unmistakable sound of a classic vespa was getting louder. Mari could see the smoke from the exhaust first. Her father got closer on the same scooter that she was taken home on after she was born.

She waved her arms at him as he came into sight, and moments later, he came to a gentle stop next to her. She threw her arms around him, and, despite the cigarette between his lips, she kissed him on both cheeks. She jumped onto the seat behind him, and he rode the last 300 metres to where the rest of the breakfast party sat.

Steve watched the old man pull the scooter up on to its stand and spent the next five minutes hugging and kissing his family. Eventually, it was Steve's turn. He was welcomed with a kiss on each cheek and a hug as if he had been spared his life.

The old man was shorter than Steve imagined. He had at least four days growth of whiskers, and his complexion reminded Steve of an old prune that had been left out in the sun for too long.

He smelt of tobacco and had a cigarette behind one ear. His bald head had nicotine stains above the ears. Steve wondered if that was where he kept his smokes even if they had been lit.

The old man spoke in Greek to his family before turning to Steve to ask, in perfect English, if they had a good crossing. Steve was at a loss for words, and Mari was laughing at his priceless reaction. She hadn't told him her father was in the Greek merchant navy and had travelled the world many times.

The old man used the name Colin if he was dealing with people speaking English, but his real name was Costas. There were so many men in their family with that name that Colin became his preferred choice.

Colin admitted to Steve that he now preferred the simple life. He loved to work on their land and owned a good number of olive trees.

Later that morning, he openly admitted that, since losing his wife and sons, he liked to drink because it helped with the pain.

He pulled Mari into his arms and said he was so happy she had done so well: a good profession and, at last, she had met a good man. Colin pulled a small flask out of his ragged trousers and proposed a toast to his beautiful daughter and her partner. "Yammas!" he shouted and took a big gulp from the flask. Thankfully, Dimitris drove Steve and Mari the half an hour from Benitses to Messonghi, and they both appreciated a decent car ride after the last few trips.

Steve had imagined the house as being like a cow shed. He couldn't have been more wrong.

They drove into Messonghi Village and turned along the coast road towards Boukari. Moments later, the car slowed and turned between two huge steel ornate gates and parked on what looked like a piece of waste land. It was the back garden, but the grass had not been cut for months.

The house in front of them had certainly seen better days; the walls of the large, detached house had, at some time been, painted white, pink, and blue. Most of the paint was now peeling off the exterior walls, exposing the grey rendering.

Colin rode his scooter past the car and rested it against the house before picking up one of the cases and heading towards the building.

Steve looked at the concrete open stone staircase which ran up the side of the house. It lead to a bare shell. The house had only been half built. Forgetting the real reason he was in Corfu, he was thinking how nice the house could look if he could have spent some money on it. It took a couple of seconds to realise what he was thinking.

Walking around to the front of the building, the first thing he noticed was the sea. It was straight in front of him. The garden, which lead from the back of the house to the beach, was surprisingly beautiful.

The grass was immaculate, and there was a path that went from the porch of the house to a gate at the end of the garden. Either side of the gate was a white wall around a metre high, which marked the border.

Steve walked to the gate and looked out to sea. He could see the mountains of mainland Greece 25km away. The sea was calm, although a breeze was blowing the few olive trees in the garden. Turning his back on the sea and looking at the house, he saw Mari was opening the huge green shutters. She waved at him and beckoned him to help her.

Colin and Dimitris were sitting on an old bench on the porch, which stretched the width of the building. They were both drinking something from a shot glass. Colin handed Steve a heavily stained mug. Another toast was called, and the contents of the mug hit the back of Steve's throat, making him cough. The two men burst out laughing just as Mari appeared. She scolded the men and apologised to Steve for her father's home made Raki.

Mari took his hand and lead him into the house. It took a few moments for his eyes to adjust to the light, but it was the smell that hit him. It was a mixture of damp, cigarette smoke, and rotten grapes. Mari noticed the look on his face and smiled.

She told him that he would get used to the smell and took him by the hand and lead him to the corner of the room. Beside a huge dark wooden bookcase, there was a door. It looked to him like a cupboard. As it opened, the smell became stronger. Mari led him down the stone staircase into a dimly lit room.

Steve couldn't believe what he was looking at. The old man had his own distillery. There were hundreds or even thousands of bottles stacked up in the cellar. These were next to the pipes, barrels, and all sorts of things he had never seen before. The cellar was larger than the house above it. Mari explained that the man who built it was obsessed with the thought of nuclear war. The shelter was supposed to be a nuclear bunker, but no one wanted to tell him it was the worst place to build such a shelter because of the sea. They watched for three years as he dug alone with a single shovel.

Mari showed Steve around the rest of the house. None of the interior walls had their original paint, and the furniture was mostly made of olive wood. It was dark and very heavy. Eventually, the two of them joined her father and Dimitris on the balcony for another shot of Raki.

It is traditional to have a siesta in Corfu, and Steve needed it. His head was spinning, and he felt quite sick. They had arranged to go back to Dimitris's restaurant that evening. He lay on the bed and tried to focus on the picture of Saint Spyridon to make the room stop spinning. It didn't work, and, moments later, he threw open the green shutters, leaned out of the window, and vomited.

Two old women walking past the house stopped to watch. They were very vocal. Steve assumed they were hurling abuse at him, but he waved at them, closed the shutters, and got back in the bed. Within seconds, he was asleep.

Mari sat on the balcony with the men. She was telling them about Bournemouth and how, only a few days ago, Steve had been in hospital.

Colin was concerned for his daughter. He had hoped she would fall in love with a banker or lawyer, but, upon finding out Steve was an out of work mechanic, he was disappointed. A few moments later, he asked her if Steve could fix the slow puncture on his scooter.

The two men laughed loudly.

Chapter 90

Sally knew the trip should take around three hours. What she didn't allow for was the traffic on the M25.

She worked out that she had done less than three miles in the last half hour and knew she would be late.

Driving a lot faster than usual, she made up at least ten minutes. The signs to Southampton indicated another twenty miles to go. She pushed the accelerator a little further. Watching the speedometer, she eased off at 96mph and switched the cruise control on.

Moments later, she noticed the flashing blue lights in her rearview mirror. Her heart began to beat faster, and she knew the penalty for being caught at this speed. The consequences could be severe for her.

She braked slightly and watched the speed of the car reduce to the legal limit of 70mph.

The police car passed her at what she thought was well over 100mph, and she watched as it disappeared out of sight. Switching the cruise control back on at 68mph, she breathed a huge sigh of relief.

It took ten minutes to find a parking space and then five more minutes to find some loose change under the seat for the parking machine.

The reception area was huge. She spoke to the receptionist who then called the ward where Sandra was. The detective had been there over an hour waiting for Sally.

Detective Mick Smallwood met Sally in the reception area. She was relieved to see he had a kind face and spoke to her in a gentle manor.

He showed her into a private room near the reception and offered her a drink.

Sally answered the same questions she had answered on the phone.

Detective Smallwood wouldn't give Sally too many more details about Sandra's injuries. He said she was in an induced coma as there had been a severe head wound, and she had a broken leg, hip, ribs, and some internal injuries.

Sally couldn't explain to the detective the reason for hers being the only number called on the mobile found in Sandra's bag. She knew why but chose not to say.

The detective then asked Sally if she would go with him to the ward and confirm Sandra's identity.

Sally felt sick as they walked into the ward. The bleeps from the monitors were the first thing she noticed. She was surprised how many nurses there were.

They then entered another room where, in front of her, she could see Sandra.

Sally could not stop the tears in her eyes.

Sandra lay motionless. It had been a while since they had been together. Sally looked at the lifeless body in front of her. There was a mask over her face and tube in her mouth and another up her nose.

There was a dressing covering half of her face and head. Her arms were outside the covers, and Sally noticed how brown they looked.

She stood looking at the woman she had once loved so much. Tears ran down her cheeks as she remembered the early innocent days they spent together. She wondered where it all had gone so wrong.

Sally reached out and put her hand on Sandra's. Her skin felt cold and made Sally shudder.

One of the monitors began to beep. Sally jumped back as one of the nurses pressed a button, and the noise stopped.

The ward sister walked over and asked them both to leave. Two minutes later, they were back in the room next to the reception.

The detective asked Sally about Sandra's work, if there was a boyfriend, and if there was anyone who was related to her.

Sally realised that things were worse than she thought and decided to tell the detective about Sandra's mother. She gave him an address and hoped she was doing the right thing.

Chapter 91

Claire was in the front garden of her little bungalow. Despite it being November, the weather was good. There was always plenty to do, and the garden was her life. If she wasn't tending to her beloved plants, she could sit in the window and watch the waves crashing onto the shingle beach.

She looked over the white wooden picket fence at the view. Every day was different. The small port of West Bay usually looked quiet this time of year, but, today, there were people walking around. Some were walking their dogs, some were fishermen were unloading their day's catch. It was unusual for a car to drive along the unmade road towards her house. It was usually a lost tourist. The two occupants of the car were looking at the names of the houses. They stopped as soon as they saw "Cliff View".

The men got out of the car and walked towards the gate.

The two officers stood in the lounge; they were both looking out at the view when Claire walked in with three mugs of tea before sitting in her armchair by the window.

She had dreaded that this day would come and calmly listened as she was told of her daughter's accident.

She had always kept her emotions to herself. This had come about due to a life of emotional turmoil. Claire once told her neighbour that she had no tears left in her body.

She had a very tough childhood; her father had always resented her as he wanted a son, and, when Claire's mother nearly died giving birth to her, he had wanted to get rid of her.

When she became pregnant with Sandra, she was seventeen years old. Her father beat her, and she was thrown out of the house with just £5. She went to live in Wales with an aunt until she was in her early twenties when she returned to look after her mother when her father was killed in an accident at work in Portsmouth docks.

She listened as she was told Sandra was very ill. Explaining to the police officers that she had not seen her daughter for many years, they seemed surprised that Claire declined the offer of a ride to Southampton to see her.

Claire told them she would catch a train the following week. Reluctantly, they left her sitting in her chair, looking out of the window at the sea.

As she sat there, motionlessly staring out at the horizon, her heart was broken again. Holding her beloved grey cat in her arms, she felt a single tear leave her right eye.

Chapter 92

Mari and Steve sat on the old scooter. It took them forty minutes to get to the restaurant, and, despite the wheels on the machine not being completely round or in line with each other, an almost flat rear tyre, the lack of brakes or speedometer, and enough smoke to cover their tracks, he was falling in love with the machine and Corfu life.

Dimitris had prepared a Greek mezze, a mixture of Sofrito, Souvlaki, Gyros, salads, fresh fish, olives, oils and fresh bread.

The local produce was washed down with plenty of Mythos beer, and, by the end of the evening, the two of them were bursting at the seams. Thankfully, one of the waiters gave them a lift back to the house on his way home. Steve looked at his watch as he climbed onto the bed. It was nearly 3 am.

Chapter 93

07/11 - 5 DAYS TO DIE DAY

Steve hadn't slept too well; the air was damp, and the mosquitos were making the most of new blood on the menu.

He managed to creep out of bed and through to the kitchen. Taking a carton of orange juice out of the fridge, he opened the kitchen door. To his surprise, he could see Colin painting the wall at the end of the garden.

The sun had not yet broken behind the Greek mountains, and the old man was working.

Steve walked up the path and, within minutes, was sitting next to Colin with a brush in his hand.

The old man explained that the best time to do any work outside in the summer was to do it before the sun rose. He also preferred the mornings. Steve reminded his new painting partner it was November and nearly winter. The old man looked at him and laughed aloud.

The house side of the wall was finished just as the sun broke through. Then the two of them sat on the porch and watched as the sky turned from red to blue.

Mari did a wonderful breakfast for the three of them, and they sat watching fishermen returning with their catch and listening to the calm sea in front of them as they ate it.

Later that morning, the restaurant waiter picked Steve and Mari up on his way to work so they could pick up the scooter.

On their way back towards Messonghi, Mari showed Steve the way up to the Achilleion Palace.

Built for the Empress Elisabeth of Austria as a refuge after losing her son in 1890, the stunning building boasted some of the finest period pieces on the island.

The views stretch north to Corfu Town and across the whole of the southern tip of Corfu into the Ionian Sea.

Mari led Steve around, and he was surprised of how much of the island's history she knew. It was like having his own personal guide. As they stood in the stunning gardens under the statue of Achilles, he couldn't resist putting his finger in front of her lips to hush her. He held her head in his hands and kissed her. She was his goddess, and he loved her so much. He wanted to make sure the next few days were the best she would ever experience.

Later that afternoon, Steve sat on the porch of the house and watched Mari as she swam in the sea. Knowing what was to happen to him in a few days made him feel sick.

Chapter 94

A nurse sat in the chair next to Sandra's bed. She was writing the notes up from her shift. Two patients had been transferred out of the ward, and this was generally a good sign. Sadly, another of the patients had passed away, a woman in her 90's knocked over by a bicycle in town. She had only been on the ward one day.

Sandra was now their biggest concern. The doctors had taken more blood and requested another scan. She was also showing signs of acute kidney failure. There could have been several causes for this. The doctors were very concerned as her breathing had become shallow, and it was probable that there was a build-up of fluid on her lungs.

The next 72 hours were critical. Sandra was in the best of hands.

Chapter 95

Claire sat in her chair, looking at a large rowing boat. She counted ten people onboard who were working together to power the boat through the breaking waves. She knew the water would have been very cold and admired anyone with the determination and stamina crazy enough to be out on the water on such a cold morning.

She was still undecided if she wanted to visit the hospital.

Remembering the last time they had met, she couldn't understand or accept her daughter's choice of company and knew that money was never going to be an issue. The two of them had a huge argument, and Sandra had slapped her mother and said she never wanted to see her again.

Despite everything, Sandra was still her daughter, and she loved her.

Chapter 96

Mari walked into the village to arrange a rental car; there was no way they could see the island on her father's scooter. Half an hour later, she parked the little Toyota on the grass alongside the house. The newly borrowed independence opened up the whole of Corfu to them, and Mari knew the best places to go.

That evening, they walked into the village where they sat in a small taverna on the beach, eating chicken Souvlaki, Steve's new favourite meal. It took five minutes to walk back to the house, and the two of them sat on the porch listening to the waves gently breaking on the beach in front of them. Colin had gone into the village to play backgammon. He used his Raki as his betting stake, and it was usual for him to return home as late as 3 am with empty bottles and singing at the top of his voice.

Mari and Steve made the most of him being out and made love on the balcony.

Chapter 97

Steve was woken at 2:30 by Colin was singing, "I want to break free" in Greek. He thought it was funny at first, but on the fourth rendition, he wished the old man would shut up.

The mosquitoes had taken a real liking to him, and along with the humidity in the room, his legs were itching like hell. He slipped out of bed and opened the shutters to get some air in the room. Thankfully, there was a slight breeze, but this also gave the mosquitos greater access to him.

He lay on top of the bed, listening to the insects and falling back asleep. An hour later, the cockerel in the neighbour's field decided it was time for everyone to wake up. Soon after that, he heard a goat bleating. That was enough for him so he crept out of the bedroom in hope that Colin who was painting something.

Chapter 98

Sally had been awake since 5 am. She sat in her office and was shredding pictures. She had already filled one sack, and there were at least a thousand more photographs to dispose of.

There were several things she needed to do. One of them was to look through the property pamphlets on her desk. She had been advised to buy another house by her bank manager. The other alternative was to let the cottage out and rent a more expensive home. There was a stunning property in Beaulieu village available, but the idea of spending £3k a month on renting scared her. However, she trusted his advice. The other thing she needed to do was to visit Sandra.

Chapter 99

As the sun peeked over the horizon Steve could smell the bread warming up in the oven and the fresh coffee percolating on the wood-fired stove.

It was hard to believe it was November and harder to comprehend was what was going to happen to him in four days.

Mari brought a coffee out to Steve; he was sitting on the bench, watching Colin tying up the beautiful wisteria that was trailing along the fence on the right-hand side of the garden.

The old man seemed to have found his place; the most important things to him were his garden and his family. Twenty years ago, Colin was well-respected. He had spent most of his life at sea and worked hard to become captain. He loved the long-term voyages and spent many years on container ships.

He was especially proud of his family. His wife looked after the home and beautiful gardens, and his sons were the apple of his eye. They had both done exceptionally well in their studies. The eldest, Giannis, was a dentist in Athens, while his younger son, Andreas, was studying in Athens to be a teacher.

Mari was just finishing school in Corfu and was hoping to be a nurse. The boys rarely visited their parents together, but Colin's birthday brought the family together. There was a family meal at Dimitri's taverna that went on until the early hours. The boys decided to return to the house, while Colin, Maeve, and Mari stayed.

The boy's car was hit head on. The driver of the other car also died. The investigation found the other driver was more than five times over the alcohol limit. Neither of the boys had been drinking as they were due back in Athens the following day. Unfortunately, neither of them had been wearing a safety belt and were killed instantly.

Maeve took the news of her sons' deaths badly. She cried for months and never seemed to get over it; she died less than a year later.

Colin returned to work two days after the funeral and was discovered to be drunk while at the helm of a ship.

This cost him his job, and he would never work again. Much of his savings were used to help Mari in her education. He loved his daughter, and she made him very proud.

Steve sat with the old man on the bench and listened to him talking about his sons. He knew that he regretted what had happened and hated the idea of Mari having to help him financially.

Mari had made a packed lunch and planned to take Steve on a road trip to the south of the Island. There were some beautiful villages up in the hills where you could see the whole of the southern tip of Corfu.

Two hours later, the car pulled up on a windy road near Chlomos. The view, as she promised, was staggering. In the distance was mainland Greece and the port of Igoumenitsa, the gateway to the rest of Greece.

They could also see Lake Korission and Halikouna Beach just below them. Mari hoped there would still be some flamingos on the lake.

There were only a handful left, wading in the shallow water that had originally been salt flats. To Steve's disappointment, they weren't bright pink. The food they ate had an influence on their colouring, and, although the food was plentiful on the lake, it lacked the shrimp colour they needed.

Driving a little further, they got to the beach. All the kiosks were closed for the winter, but there were still some sunbeds on the beach. Steve sat and watched Mari as she braved the cooler water and swam.

Steve had formulated a plan for D Day. He wanted the two of them to be alone. He had thought long and hard about how he was going to get shot. He didn't own a gun and, as far as he knew, neither did Mari.

There was still an element of doubt in his mind, but he needed to be prepared.

Steve knew Mari had wanted to take him to Paxos but didn't fancy the idea of being with a boat full of strangers on his last day. Instead, he was hoping her uncle Costas, who worked at a brokerage company in Corfu Town, could help them.

Mari walked towards him, and it reminded him of Ursula Andress in the film Dr. No.

She looked amazing with the seawater dripping off her olive skin. He couldn't help but notice her goose pimples. She was cold. He stood up and wrapped a towel around her as she sat with him on the sunbed. He wrapped his arm around her and rubbed her back for warmth.

Chapter 100

As Sally drove towards the hospital, she tried to plan how the conversation may go. It didn't occur to her that Sandra may not be fit enough to talk to her.

Walking towards the ward, she felt tense, her heart was beating faster, and her mouth became dry. She approached the nurse station and asked the nurse behind the desk if she could see Sandra. Sally was told to wait for the ward sister.

A tall, thin woman with jet-black hair approached and asked Sally if she was a relation.

Sally explained that she had visited a couple of days ago with Detective Smallwood, and they were permitted to see Sandra. The sister then asked Sally to follow her.

Instead of going into the recovery room where Sandra was, they walked into a small office. The door was closed behind them, and the sister explained that Sandra was very ill.

The damage to her internal organs were much worse than they originally thought. She was now critical, and, for the next few days, she was being kept in isolation to prevent any chance of infection.

As Sally drove out of the car park, she saw a woman cross the road in front of her.

Despite not seeing her for years, she thought she recognised Sandra's mother Claire, looking much older than she remembered. Sally was sure it was her.

Claire had always looked young. Sally had wondered why her own mother never looked as trendy. Sandra shared her clothes with her mother, and, often, they were mistaken as sisters.

Sally drove on towards home.

It took Claire a taxi ride, two trains, and a bus route to get to Southampton Hospital.

She hated going anywhere on her own and preferred to stay close to home.

She had become a recluse and saw no benefit in having friends. She was very content with her own company and her life. She looked at the bush outside the entrance to the hospital and felt sorry for it. It had been neglected for months and would probably end up in a skip. She wished she could take it home and nurture it back to health. "Ironic," she thought, "considering I'm standing outside the building that represents care."

She walked in and up to the large reception desk where a young girl with a tattoo on her forearm asked if she could help. Claire was given instructions of how to get to the Intensive Care Unit on the fourth floor.

A few minutes later, she was asking another nurse. This she did another five times until eventually she stood in front of the electric sliding door.

A passing nurse noticed her looking petrified and standing still like a statue.

"Are you ok?" she asked.

There was no answer, and the nurse put her hand on Claire's arm, which made her jump.

She told the nurse whom she had come to see.

It was obvious to anyone that the poor woman was in shock. She was shown to a seat just behind her; the nurse pressed the entry button and went into the ward. Moments later, she returned with a man who looked more like a solicitor than a doctor. He introduced himself and asked Claire to follow him.

The nurse helped Claire up and, holding on to her arm, guided her to a room just a little further up the corridor.

Sitting in the family room, the doctor introduced himself again. He could see the poor woman was not at all comfortable with her surroundings and seemed confused. He asked for her name and for whom did she come to see.

Satisfied with her answers, he slid a plastic chair in front of her and sat down.

Claire listened to every word without saying anything.

"I'm so sorry madam," he began.

"Your daughter's condition is very serious; she has a bad head injury, and, unfortunately, there was a bleed on her brain. We will not be able to tell how much, if any damage, may have been done. She is in an induced coma at the moment; it is the best way to help her recover as quickly as possible"

Claire looked at the doctor, and he was unsure of how much she understood. He continued.

"Your daughter has some internal injuries that we are hoping with the right medication will improve."

The doctor asked if Claire understood what he was saying. She looked at him and nodded.

She didn't say a word as he continued to tell her about the complications with her lungs and kidneys.

The three of them sat in silence for a few minutes. The nurse broke the silence by offering her a cup of tea. This prompted the biggest response. Claire looked at her and said, "Please."

The mug of tea was scolding hot, but that did not stop her from sipping it loudly.

As she sat on the train, Claire stared out of the window at the deer in the New Forest; she felt numb. The thought of her daughter dying had never crossed her mind. Despite all their differences, she loved Sandra with all her heart. It was Sandra that had caused her so much pain, anxiety, and worry. She wondered, for a moment, if she would be better dead. Within seconds, she regretted the thought.

Claire had other thoughts on her mind, thoughts which could have a far-reaching serious impact should she act on them. She decided to wait and see what the doctors had to say in 24 hours. As the train pulled into Christchurch station, she remembered standing on the platform many years ago with the only man she loved. There had never been another in her life.

Robert was the only man she had ever wanted.

Chapter 101

Mari drove the car in through the gates into the unkept rear garden and came to a sudden stop. She flung the door open and ran up to the scooter laying on its side, Colin was laying under the machine. Steve wasn't far behind her and they lifted the scooter off the old man. He was so drunk he didn't even wake up when they carried him inside and lay him on the sofa.

The two of them prepared a Greek salad together and sat on the balcony to eat it. There was a boat going to Corfu Town later that afternoon and Mari had arranged for them to go, an hour later Colin walked into the back garden, he muttered something in Greek to Mari and sat in his garden chair, he was snoring in less than two minutes. Mari threw a blanket over him as they left to walk into the village.

The boat took an hour from Messonghi to Corfu Town, the air was chilly, but Steve was happy to wear shorts and a sweatshirt, Mari had a big puffer jacket and jeans on, she knew how cold it could get after dark.

The two of them walked around the old town. The timeless lanes were quiet, in the summer all the shops would be open and the tourists making the most of the good value leather goods and looking in the many trinket shops and Jewellers.

Mari stopped to look in the window of one where she spotted a beautiful gold and diamond ring, she looked lovingly at the piece,

Steve could see the sparkle in her eyes and made a mental note of the name above the shop.

Some of the restaurants were still open and Mari was taking Steve to one of her favourites.

The Liston has a venetian appearance, the arcaded terraces are made out of the traditional stone and was built in the early 1800's. It housed many fashionable cafes and restaurants. Not all of them were open but Mari knew the one they were heading for opened all year.

As they walked in one of the waiters recognised Mari. He walked over and kissed her on both cheeks, she introduced him to Steve and the two of them shook hands.

Steve tried not to flinch, the man had the strongest grip ever experienced and not wanting to seem rude he tried to release his grip, it felt an age before Steve's throbbing hand was released.

Mari explained the waiter was her cousin, it was his father that sold luxury yachts.

On hearing this Steve decided her cousin could shake his hand whenever he liked. After the meal, they wandered around the almost deserted town, they saw three other people in the next half an hour, and they all knew Mari.

They decided to sit inside the boat on its return journey to Messonghi, the air was much cooler and Steve was wishing he had his jacket and jeans on as well.

Steve spoke to Costas junior, Mari's cousin, he wanted to ask if there were any more men in the family named Costas, but more importantly he wanted to arrange to meet his father to see if they could charter a boat so the two of them could go to Paxos.

Colin was still asleep in the big garden chair when they arrived home, Mari checked on him and judging by the snoring he was happy.

Steve lay in bed listening to Mari snoring as well, it seemed as soon as she breathed out he could hear Colin in the garden breathe in. He wondered if he would get any sleep, thinking about the boat trip did the job and a while later they were all snoring.

Chapter 102

09/11 – 3 DAYS TO DIE DAY

As they drove towards Corfu port, Steve was thinking that if there were no boats for hire, he could buy one. He had no idea how much they were and thinking more along the lines of car prices, he hoped they could find something for £25k.

They drove into the yard. Costas Sr. was standing outside the office door.

He was a big man, almost as wide as tall he had a mass of black hair that was swept back.

His brown face and thick black monobrow made him look like a wrestler. Steve didn't expect the man to speak English as well as he did, and he certainly didn't expect the man to have such a loud voice.

Mari almost disappeared into the man's cleavage as he wrapped his arms around her, she looked very relieved as he let her go. Steve suspected he knew what the man's handshake would be like, he wasn't wrong, tears welled up in his eyes as his hand was being crushed.

The two of them were guided over towards one of the most beautiful boats Steve had ever seen. Costas gave him a brochure, and, as they got closer, Steve began to sweat. It wasn't the heat of the sun but the price on the top of the piece of paper.

Beneteau, Gran Turismo, 49.15.73m 6 Birth, 3 cabins, two Volvo 435bhp engines, the price: 420,000 Euros.

Costas boarded first, Mari followed, and Steve stood motionless on the dock. His knees felt weak. He was speechless and was in love.

It took a few moments to realise he was being laughed at. He was sure the booming laugh from Costas was echoing around the harbour.

To his disappointment, Costas told Steve the boat had been sold.

Steve had gone from being apprehensive to excited then disappointed in a millisecond. The best was saved until last. Costas announced he was delivering the boat to its new owner on Paxos in three days, and Mari and Steve could go along for the ride.

The next three hours were spent sitting at the table on the back of the boat, eating and drinking. There was a fully stacked bar on board, including a case of San Miguel.

The boat was a fantasy. Never in his wildest dreams could Steve have afforded to run the boat, even if he could afford to buy it.

Costas promised once they were underway and clear of the harbour, Steve could take the controls. On hearing this, Steve almost said,

"What a way to die."

Mari drove home, and Steve slept in the passenger seat. He had drunk nearly every bottle of beer in the case and was feeling a little drunk when they got into the car.

It was dark by the time they got back to the house. Colin's scooter was gone. Then Mari remembered him telling her he was staying at Dimitri's that evening. They had the house to themselves.

Steve was almost dragged into the house. Mari got him to the bedroom and dumped his body on the bed. He didn't move all night.

Chapter 103

Claire spent most of the day in the garden. There was a heavy mist in the bay, and it brought important moisture to the plants. It had been such a mild autumn, the garden still looked beautiful. The grass was perfectly cut with visible lines, and the borders were weed free. Whenever possible, Claire would spend every daylight minute outside.

The fresh air cleared her head, and there was so much to think about. The hospital should have called, but the phone never rang. This made her feel more anxious, but she assumed if things had gotten worse, the doctor would have called.

It was getting dark, and it was almost time for her favourite quiz show on TV. She cleared up and put the tools in her shed.

The best time of the day, according to her, was the morning. The alarm always went off at 4:45 am. Because of this, she would always be in bed by 9:30pm. This night was no exception. At exactly 9:30, she climbed into bed and read for half an hour. It was generally a book about flowers or gardening, and, at 10 pm, she would listen to the news on Radio 4 before switching off the light.

At 10:35 pm, the house phone rang. Claire didn't hear it.

Chapter 104

Steve woke with the worse hangover he had ever had. Colin tried to get him to drink a glass of Raki, but the smell made him feel worse.

Walking out on to the porch, he could see Mari. He thought she was mad, swimming in the sea this time of year. He walked through the gate at the end of the garden and on to the beach. He was the only person there.

Steve hated swimming. He fell into a pond when he was five years old, and, although it was only six inches deep, it had frightened him so much that the fear of water had never left him.

"There had never been a better time to face your fears; when your life clock is ticking you need to push yourself."

Steve remembered hearing this on a Radio 4 programme a few weeks ago. The presenter was talking to a woman who was terminally ill. Despite her condition, she managed to do a tandem sky dive.

Thinking of how that must have felt, Steve kicked off his flip-flops, took his shorts off, and walked naked towards the water.

Mari had lied to him. The water was freezing. He stood there with nothing on up to his ankles in the calm water. He thought he was going to get frost bite and was terrified of the water going any further up his legs.

He could see Mari swimming as fast as she could towards him, and, as she stood up in the shallow water, he noticed she was also naked.

Not wanting to seem a complete wimp he took a few more steps. The water was now inching towards his groin. Gritting his teeth and swearing quietly, he took one more step.

Mari knew he hated swimming, and she felt immensely proud of him as he walked towards her. She thought he would have been swearing aloud with every step and was about to walk closer when he disappeared.

He had no idea what he stood on. It was likely to have been a small rock. It was enough to make his legs give way. His whole body went under the water, the freezing water.

Blind panic set in along with the shock of being submerged. He had taken a mouthful of the finest salty Ionian Sea. Standing up as quick as possible, Mari was standing in front of him. She threw her arms around him. She had no idea that his submersion had been accidental. To her it looked as if he was being brave.

The two of them walked further into the water, and the deeper they went, the cooler it became. Not wanting to go any further than his shoulders, the both stood still. The cool air on Steve's face made him realise that the water was warmer than he thought. It was the air that was cold. Mari wrapped her arms around his neck and they kissed.

Looking inland, he could see the house and the village of Chlomos perched up high in the luscious green hills and, behind them, the Greek Mainland Mountains that stretched towards the sky. It would not be long before the snow fell on them and the Greek ski resorts became full for another winter.

A while later, they were drying themselves off in the warmth of the house. The winds had changed, and large clouds were building on the horizon. Colin was dragging his big chair towards the small stone outhouse where he kept his gardening tools. Steve went to help him while Mari put some fresh coffee on the stove.

The thunder announced its intentions. The air pressure changed, and, out at sea, the rain created a vertical wall of water that was coming their way. Colin walked into the house as the first drops began to fall. The shutters on most of the windows had been securely fastened, and a large empty bucket was placed in the middle of the room where there was a small hole in the roof.

A single clap of thunder shook the house. The sky darkened, and the heavens opened. Steve stood watching the rain out of the only open window. He had never seen anything like it. The wall at the end of the garden had become invisible. A waterfall was cascading over the balcony, which created a rumble of its own as it hit the wood on the porch floor.

The rain showed no sign of easing off, and an hour later, the lights flickered and went out.

Power cuts were a regular occurrence on the Island, and people were always prepared with candles and torches. Colin produced four oil lamps, and, when they were lit, the atmosphere in the house seemed different. They made everything seem older. It may have been the smell as well, but it felt as if they had been transported back in time.

Steve was conscious of the time he was losing. He wished for only one thing, the one thing money could not buy: time.

At 11 pm, the rain stopped. Mari was asleep, and Steve lay wide-awake, listening to Colin singing.

Chapter 105

Claire sat at the dining table, holding a cup of tea she made three hours ago. The phone startled her as it rang again, causing some of the tea to spill onto the tablecloth. She counted the rings. This time it was thirteen.

It was late in the afternoon, and she was still wearing her dressing gown.

The Daily Mail crossword sat in front of her. Normally, she would have it done in 30 minutes, but there was only one answer filled in with a pencil and an attempt to erase it with her wet finger.

The phone calls began at 9:30 and had rung nearly every two hours since.

Despite the dining table being in the middle of her living room, Claire could still see the waves. It was a typically miserable November's day. It had been raining when she woke, and, according to the television weather report, it wouldn't stop for another 24 hours.

Her stomach had been rumbling for hours, but she had no appetite for food.

Desperate to go to the bathroom, she struggled to stand. Leaning on the table, she pushed herself up, but her hand slipped on the tablecloth.

She fell to the floor, hitting her head hard on the carpet. As she lay there, the cold tea dripped off the edge of the table and was forming a puddle next to her. She watched it soaking in to the cream fibres and slowly closed her eyes.

The doorbell rung, and there was no answer. WPC Mel Saunders switched on her torch. Her colleague sat in the car, sheltering from the rain and thankful he picked heads when they flipped the coin.

He saw the beam of light through the rain and watched as his partner stood in the middle of the wet flowerbed, peering through the window.

Moments later, he heard her calling for him.

They could clearly see someone laying on the floor inside, and Mel walked round to the back of the house. The rear door opened into the kitchen. The first thing that she noticed was how cold the room was. Using her torch to find the switch, she turned the light on and noticed the window was wide open.

The rain had soaked everything within its reach. A beautiful but very wet grey cat was sitting on the draining board. It looked at her and meowed loudly.

Mel called out, and she heard a faint moan as she walked into the lounge. Her young partner followed moments later.

Claire looked at the policewoman who was kneeling next to her. She heard a man's voice asking for an ambulance and immediately began to object, trying to sit up.

Mel was trying to keep the old woman still. She had not had a chance to assess the situation and see if there were any visible serious injuries. She could feel the lady was cold, very cold.

Claire insisted on being helped to sit up. Now more conscious of her situation, she told Mel she had only fallen. It took both officers to help her to the sofa where there were some blankets to wrap around her.

Mel held a glass of water as Claire sipped it. She felt so stupid, and although she insisted she was ok, an ambulance was on its way.

The paramedics sat with Claire. Although she had a large bump on her head, she seemed ok. Their main concern was her obvious confusion and low temperature. She was visibly very dehydrated.

Despite her objections, Claire was told she had to go to hospital. She agreed to go after Mel promised that she would personally look after the cat.

Claire was taken to Dorchester Hospital and was seen immediately. She had been put on a drip to rehydrate her and had a heart monitor beside the bed that was silently displaying her output. She felt completely exhausted and eventually fell asleep at 3 am. Looking at her notes, the nurse saw several elderly patients this time of year with pneumonia, but this patient looked younger.

Chapter 106

11/11 DIE TOMORROW

Steve was awake early as he needed to ask Colin a huge favour. When Mari looked out, the two of them were sitting in the garden in deep conversation. It made her feel so happy.

The rain had made everything in the garden smell good, and the air was much fresher. The two men also discussed the weather, and Steve was pleased to find out there was no more rain due for another three days.

Mari prepared breakfast for the three of them. She was planning to take Steve to the north of the island, and she wanted to take him to two of the most beautiful places on the island, Agni and Kassiopi.

Mari heard her father ride off on his scooter. The distinct sound of its noisy engine and the rattle of bottles in the basket tied to the seat made her assume he had an appointment with a backgammon board. She looked out of the window and smiled as she saw a plume of smoke heading towards the village.

Half an hour later, they drove towards Corfu Town. Steve loved the journey. The road hugged the east coast of the island. As they passed through Benitses, she leaned on the car horn. Dimitri's taverna already looked busy with customers waiting for their breakfast.

Before you get into Corfu Town, the coast road climbs to a stunning viewpoint. Mari saw a space and stopped.

Standing on a small terrace, the view looks over the 11th century Chapel on Mouse Island, the airport, harbour, fort, and town. Photographed by millions of people over the years, the view is one of Corfu's most used and loved.

Once past the main town, the road passes the big port and climbs again. The views across to the mainland and to Albania just kept getting better.

Eventually, Mari took a small right turn and drove down one of the steepest hills. Steve had been down in a car. After parking, they walked five minutes to the bay of Agni.

The tiny deserted bay was surrounded by huge slopes on each side, which added to the dramatic feel. The small jetty's hosts hundreds of boats in the summer and multi- million pound yachts anchor offshore. Their owners use their small dinghies to get to the busy tavernas.

Sitting on the end of the jetty, they could hear the waves lapping gently at the shore. Steve understood why this little cove meant so much to Mari.

Chapter 107

Sally sat in the car outside the huge ornate metal gates. She was waiting for the estate agent who promised to meet her there.

She looked at her watch for the fifth time that minute. Then she heard a car driving towards her. The gates swung inwards, and Sally realised she was blocking the lane. A large Bentley pulled towards her and forced her to reverse into a small alcove. Her car came to a sudden halt as she heard the unmistakable sound of the back of it hitting something hard.

Without even a wave of thanks, the Bentley sped past her, and, as a gesture of thanks, she wound down the window and stuck her fingers up at the disappearing car.

Standing in front of her within the gates stood the estate agent, a tall skinny-looking man with a suit too small for him and the biggest shoes she had ever seen. She put the car into first gear and drove through the gates into a large gravelled courtyard. She drove far too fast and applied the brakes as hard as she could to make two nice deep grooves in the stones. Feeling a little better, she got out of the car as the lanky man ran over to her.

The look on his face was enough to tell Sally she wanted to leave. She had seen enough of the building already, and, although she was sure it was a beautiful house, she couldn't imagine living there.

The young man swore at her and asked if she had ever driven on a gravel drive before.

She looked at the red-faced scruffy individual, and, for the second time in as many minutes, stuck her fingers up at him as well. The front wheels displaced many more pieces of stone before flying through the gates.

Ten minutes later, she pulled up outside a beautiful farmhouse. An old woman sitting on a chair outside the stable door waved and smiled. Sally had a wonderful feeling straight away.

The old woman, who introduced herself as Alice, had already shown Sally the stables and yard when the same estate agent turned up. Casually, Sally walked over to him and told him she didn't need his assistance and to kindly leave as she was going in the cottage with Alice for afternoon tea.

The man looked extremely upset as he walked back towards his car.

Alice explained that her daughter had insisted on renting the house and land. They had built a lovely little granny annex for her by the sea at their Margate House in Kent. Sally phoned Alice's daughter and began to negotiate a mutually beneficial deal.

Chapter 108

Claire woke early. Her chest felt tight, and she began to cough. For a moment, she struggled for breath. She coughed again, and her mouth filled with phlegm. she looked for something to spit in, but another cough forced the thin, watery fluid from her mouth. A moment later, a nurse stood next to her with a bowl.

Claire's breath was short. The nurse put an oxygen mask on her to help her breathe and sat her up.

As she tried to talk, another convulsion brought up more liquid. This time, it looked more red. She knew she was ill and knew she needed to leave. She had to try to get to Southampton. She had to try to see her daughter before it was too late.

The nurse watched Claire's eyes close and checked the heart monitor. Happy her patient was sleeping, she walked away.

Chapter 109

Kassiopi was busier than Mari expected. Some of the shops and tavernas were still open, and Mari's favourite was one of them.

The two of them sat sharing a huge glass of chocolate ice cream while watching a large yacht manoeuvring into a space, the crew checking to make sure they didn't damage the boats either side of them.

After a walk around the harbour, they climbed through the narrow streets until they found a little bench which overlooked the whole area.

It reminded Mari of a childhood holiday when her parents had brought her and her brothers to the north of the island. It was only for three days, but it was also the only family holiday together she remembered.

Steve was getting conscious of the time, unknown to Mari he had arranged for the two of them to go for a meal at a restaurant Colin had recommended. When Mari suggested they work their way towards home, he agreed. They had a table booked for 9:30, and it would take at least an hour and a half to get home.

Steve wore a smart teal blue polo shirt and a new pair of blue chino shorts. When Mari walked out on to the porch, his eyes lit up. She was wearing a dark blue, strapless dress. The material was tight across her bust line with a small slit of three inches between her breasts. It flowed to just above her knees. She was wearing a matching coloured pair of sandals with the clasp around her ankle. She looked perfect. Steve regretted not packing a suit. Colin stood in front of them and, using his old camera, took one picture. He looked proudly at his beautiful daughter, and she could see a tear in his eye.

A taxi picked them up at 8:30, and drove them out of the village. Driving towards Moraitika, the car turned left along a narrow road that wound its way higher and higher. Mari knew exactly where they were going.

The Archontiko Restaurant in Chlomotiana was the place where her family went to celebrate. The host was a friend of her fathers and had not seen Mari for some years.

The building perched on top of the hill has breath-taking, panoramic views over the island.

The lovely huge tables were made from polished driftwood with thick glass tops. Andreas had a table reserved for the two of them inside along with a bottle of champagne on ice.

There was so much on the menu to choose from.

Steve said very little during the main course, and Mari asked if he was alright. There was so much he wanted to say to her but was frightened that she wouldn't understand.

As soon as they finished the main course, Steve excused himself and walked towards bathroom.

Mari sat alone for a few minutes, looking around at the beautiful building and decorations. She hardly noticed the two traditionally dressed singers approaching the table. As they began to sing to her, she felt very insecure and uncomfortable. Then she noticed the lone Greek dancer with his back to her. Mari tried not to laugh, because he had no rhythm, and she thought him to be very drunk until he turned around.

Russell D Whitney

Steve was wearing the full traditional uniform of the presidential guard, complete with a red sash, white pleated foustanella and polished black shoes topped with pompons.

She didn't know if she should laugh or cry. Thankfully, the singing stopped, and Steve knelt at her feet. He looked into her eyes and produced the very ring she had seen in the Corfu Lane Jewellers; Steve began his speech.

"Mari, since you came into my life I have known love like no other. I want you to know there will never be another woman in my life, and as I present you with this token of my love, I would like to know if you will be my bride."

Mari looked up to see every guest in the restaurant standing to see what she was going to say.

Steve stood up and waited for what seemed like hours. Mari threw herself at him causing him to stumble backwards into Andreas. The room erupted in applause as they kissed.

Feeling very proud but also a complete fool, Mari made Steve wear the uniform all evening, including the journey home in the taxi.

Colin was waiting up for them and insisted the three of them have a drink to celebrate. By the time they got into bed, the two of them were feeling very delicate.

Chapter 110

Mr. G, the American king of sleaze, sat on the balcony of his Sandbanks mansion.

The man had money, dirty money. He once had a multimillion-dollar business but became greedy and didn't believe in paying taxes.

Only a few people knew he would never return to his beloved Texas since there was a million- dollar bounty on his head. He knew if he returned, his privileged lifestyle would be finished.

He still wanted to be involved in the industry but now wanted to offer a personal bespoke service for very rich clients with specific needs.

The mansion was a miniature version of the Whitehouse. He had it built in less than two years and reportedly sued the building company for £2million for completing construction two days late. It is fair to say he has more enemies than friends.

Smoking one of his legendary fat cigars, the ash was falling on to his huge stomach, and his face was blotchy from his recent trip to Spain. He hated traveling anywhere and preferred to sit under the huge sun umbrella, letting everyone come to him. He spent most of the day sitting in the same chair, smoking, eating, and drinking.

Occasionally, he would remember his beautiful wife and how good life was. These memories often ended with the smell of cordite or feeling pieces of his wife's brain on his face. He tried for years to forget what happened that day but never would.

He was still on the phone when he called out to his minder.

In a deep Texan accent, he bellowed,

"Conrad. Conrad! Conrad, come here!"

Moments later, the well-dressed, burly man stood at the table.

His instructions were quite clear.

"Go and find that bitch who has my money, I want you back in 24 hours with the pictures I asked for and my money. And remind her who I am."

Conrad knew exactly what he had to do.

Unfortunately for anyone who crossed, Mr G. the consequences were harsh.

The last woman who tried to embezzle money from the Texan needed to have two fingers amputated. Conrad had only intended to break them in the car door. The only reason she got off lightly was because he was screwing her.

Conrad himself was a child mercenary. He had spent most of his life protecting the people who looked after him. He was only fourteen when he shot his best friend for stealing from him. From that moment, he realised he had no feeling of remorse or regret. He was paid very well, but he got his satisfaction in knowing he was pleasing his boss. At times, Mr. G rewarded him in other ways.

Conrad remembered the last night he saw Sandra. He still had her silk panties in his secure locker.

He went to his room with the addresses for Sandra and her mother. He packed a small bag and made his way to the garage where eight Audi cars were parked. He stood for a moment before deciding to take the Dragon Orange Q8. He preferred the R8, but it was too flashy.

Conrad called these trips missions, he felt like James Bond and he always got the girl.

A while later, the car sped east along the Wessex Way. He managed to get two camera flashes on the road and was hoping for more on the M27. The traffic was heavy, and every time he accelerated beyond 100, another car in front slowed his car down.

One of the advantages of having a boss like his was having access to an unlimited number of driving licences. He was untraceable.

His new mobile phone rang. It was Mr. G. He told Conrad that Sandra was in Southampton Hospital. He was to go there and await another call.

Chapter 111

It was just before midnight, and the night nurse was checking on her patients. The only sounds coming from the ward were of three patients snoring loudly. They were almost in tune with each other. Bed eleven was empty. A pillow had been carefully positioned under the covers to resemble someone sleeping.

Chapter 112

12/11 – A LOVELY DAY TO DIE

Steve stood in the garden, watching the orange sunrise over the Greek mountains. There were a few light clouds, but, above them, the sky was clear and light blue, and the water in front of him was shimmering in the glow.

He was trying to look for something new. Then a fishing boat broke the orange line in the water, and he watched the man on the boat lifting pots from the seabed.

Colin was painting the beach side of the garden wall. Steve guessed he must have been out for hours making the most of the cool air.

Mari called from the kitchen, and both men walked together along the path toward the house, the smell of coffee getting stronger as they got closer.

The boat was due to leave at mid-day, and the captain of the day, Costas, had been on board since 4 am.

He was doing the final checks before their 12:00 departure. 700 euro of fuel had already been taken on board. At a speed close to 45 knots, it would consume 38 gallons an hour. To run such a beautiful vessel, the owner wouldn't worry about running costs.

There would be six people aboard on the trip to Paxos: himself, Mari, Steve, plus the owner's son and wife who were arriving by plane from the UK.

It was only 9:00 am. Costas sat at the table and listened to the shipping weather forecast on the radio. It was going to be a wonderfully smooth journey, and he intended to take a leisurely two and a half to three hours to get to Paxos.

Mari commented on how smart Steve looked. His new white and blue Crew polo shirt and blue shorts made him look like a seasoned sailor. She was wearing a tight pair of white jeans and one of Steve's sweatshirts. Mari looked at Steve and growled at him before laughing and blowing a kiss.

They eventually drove off just before 11 am, giving them just over an hour to drive the 20km to the port.

Steve was feeling anxious. He had no idea how the day was going to go. For all he knew, they could be involved in some kind of incident on the way to the port. He was now also worrying that Mari would be hurt. The hardest part was keeping his thoughts to himself.

Chapter 113

It was 8am and Sandra's nurse was standing by her bed. She was concerned that there had been little sign of improvement in the last twenty-four hours. The biggest worry now was her kidneys. They knew now that both of them had been severely damaged, and, if she were to survive, she would need constant dialysis or a transplant. The doctors had already put a request out for suitable donors.

There was still no positive output from her brain.

A ward domestic walked into the small day room. The area was mostly used by patient's families waiting to see their loved ones. There were a mixture of chairs and a new sofa donated by a local charity. An old woman was asleep, sitting on the sofa. She was holding an envelope. The cleaner tidied the magazines on the table and decided to return in an hour after the woman had woken.

Sally was sorting out files in the office when the phone rang. She answered it without looking at the number on the screen. She froze when she heard her voice.

It was Billington.

She sounded different.

Sally listened and was shocked at what she was heard.

Billington said, "I've done something very stupid."

She told Sally about going to Sandra's apartment to look for the photos of her. She also knew Sandra had sent one of the pictures to an American who lived in the Bournemouth area.

Billington explained that she was still in Paris and told Sally she had lost her job, because she had not returned to the UK.

She didn't tell Sally how she knew, but she did say she was aware that Sandra was in hospital after an accident.

She went on to tell Sally that Sandra had threatened to expose her and publish more pictures of her. This would have wrecked her professional reputation, and she would also face public humiliation. She also said Sandra had given her £20k and told her if she ever contacted Sally again, her life would be ruined.

Sally could tell Billington was sobbing as she apologised again and said she was frightened; she also knew that Sandra still had pictures of her.

Sally was trying to put the story into perspective. She knew Sandra had money. There was no reason for what had been going on.

Billington pleaded for Sally to talk to Sandra; whatever had happened between the two of them had to be sorted. Billington wanted to return home, and she wanted her job back.

Sally promised to go to the hospital and promised Billington she would see her very soon.

After the call, Sally sat in silence looking out into the garden. She remembered Steve walking past with the lawn mower and blowing her a kiss. The tears fell from her cheeks as she wished she could turn back time.

There were things she wanted to talk to Steve about. She regretted having so many secrets and wished she could tell him about the money or where it was coming from.

Life was much less complicated before her father went missing.

Chapter 114

The hospital domestic dragged the vacuum cleaner into the day room. The old lady was still sitting on the sofa with the envelope in her hand. Calling the woman as softly as she could, there was no answer. She gently reached out and touched the woman on the hand. She was cold, dead cold.

A few minutes later, there were three nurses and a doctor in the day room.

They pried the envelope out of Claire's hand and found a simple message written on the front:

"Sandra, my darling daughter. SORRY x".

The doctor looked at Claire and guessed she had been there several hours. He called security to ask for the night guards to contact him, took the envelope, and left.

He decided that only Sandra should open the letter unless she were to die.

Chapter 115

Sally drove towards Southampton. As she got closer to Beaulieu, she decided to stop off to see Alice who was in the stables brushing her beloved horse. Sally was going to take over the horse and stables when she moved in. She knew nothing about equestrian life but was keen to learn. Alice handed her a brush and lesson one began. She loved spending time with Alice and the horse. She decided to visit the hospital the following morning.

Chapter 116

Mari and Steve arrived at the port and were greeted by Costas in his usual loud manner. Steve watched her disappear between the man's arms and hoped she would survive the ordeal.

As the three of them walked towards the boat, Steve saw a couple already aboard, a young woman sitting at the table on the rear deck and a well-groomed man sitting in the pilot seat. He casually asked Costas who they were.

Looking a little embarrassed, Costas said it was the new owner's son and his wife.

As the three of them boarded the boat, the man sitting in the pilot seat said aloud.

"Excuse me, who are you?"

Steve immediately felt embarrassed and was about to answer when Costas began to explain.

He told the man it was his niece and partner from England, and they wanted to go to Paxos. Costas said it was his idea to keep him company on the journey.

The reply was to make Steve, Mari, and Costas very uncomfortable.

"There are lots of tourist boats that go to Paxos; now why don't the two of you piss off and find your own transport."

The man's wife stood and looked embarrassed by her husband's comment.

"Sheridan!" she shouted.

Steve almost burst out laughing; he wondered what type of person would call their son Sheridan. He had to bite his lip even harder when he learned her name was Cynthia.

Thankfully, Cynthia had an influence over her husband, and, after an uncomfortable few minutes, they all shook hands while Costas fetched a bottle of his brother's home brewed Raki.

Chapter 117

Conrad parked the car in the hospital car park.

Eventually, the phone rang, and Mr. G told him that a nurse would come and get him. Conrad gave his boss the registration number of the car, and the phone went dead.

Ten minutes later, a man in a white overall knocked on the window of the car. Conrad opened the window and was told he could not see Sandra. She was very ill and there was a high probability she was going to die in the next 48 hours.

Conrad was disappointed with this news. He had never failed a mission yet. He gave the nurse a £50 note and his telephone number and told him to call if her condition changed.

The Audi pulled out of the car park and headed towards the motorway. He worked out that if he put his foot down hard, he could get home in 90 minutes or sooner.

Chapter 118

As the boat pulled slowly out of Corfu harbour, the ladies sat at the table on the rear deck. Sheridan threw another tantrum because Costas wouldn't let him steer the boat out.

Steve wanted to hit the man so hard he would be out for the whole journey. Thankfully, sensibility prevailed. He was pleased the girls were getting on so well. They had opened a bottle of champagne and were enjoying the view.

The boat cleared the harbour and turned to the right. Costas called Steve to take control as he pulled in the fenders. The look on Sheridan's face was priceless; even the girls were sniggering as Costas winked and smiled at them.

On returning to the bridge of the boat, Costas took time to show Steve the computerised navigation screen and which way he should steer. They were only on half throttle, but the two 435 bhp Volvo engines burbled happily.

Sheridan eventually calmed down and approached Steve.

"Look, I'm sorry for being an arse. I'm so used to getting things my way. Can we start again?" he said. As he did so, he held out his hand.

As they shook hands, Steve thought about trying the Costas killer handshake but decided again to be the more grown up out of the two of them.

The boat passed Messonghi, and Costas pressed the impressive horn; unsurprisingly, there was no sign of life at the house.

As they approached Notos, Costas decided to stop. They were making good time, and Notos is another stunning little bay. Sheridan threw out the fenders as they glided up to the jetty. The boat came to a perfect halt, and Mari stepped off and tied up.

Despite Sheridan trying to be friendlier, he was still acting a complete arse. The more he drank, the worse he got. The five of them sat in the little taverna and the vile man insisted Cynthia take her top off to show the others her boobs. His reasoning for this was that he paid for them so he should be able to see them whenever he wanted. Cynthia ended up slapping the pompous man across the face and walking off back to the boat. Mari went off after her while Costas decided he should put the man in his place.

As the boat pulled away from the jetty, Sheridan apologised again to everyone.

As the trip progressed, Steve became more relaxed. The beers helped, but he was counting on his fingers how many hours were left in the day.

The engines were soon up to just over half throttle, and Steve was in the pilot seat again. They were making good time. They hoped to arrive in Paxos at around 2:30 to 3pm. The ladies decided to go below deck; there was a small lounge area where they could sit and talk without any men listening. Steve smiled to himself as he listened to them laughing together.

Sheridan sat on the upper deck. He was drinking champagne out of the bottle and muttering to himself. Costas went up to see if he could have a discrete word with him but returned seconds later. He looked at Steve and shrugged his shoulders.

Chapter 119

Sandra's doctor sat at his desk; the envelope found in her mother's hand was in front of him.

He picked it up and looked at it closely as if to see if he could read anything inside.

He knew that Sandra was terribly ill, and there should have been some signs of progress. Just as he was about to go and check on her, the ward sister knocked on his door and walked in.

The two of them talked about Sandra and her mother. When they found her mother, she was still wearing a wristband from Dorchester hospital. She had managed to sneak out of the ward, find a coat, and, somehow, get from Dorchester to Southampton. They assumed she used a taxi. The door to the garden in the day room was not locked. That was obviously how she got in. They also knew she had pneumonia and dementia. She was obviously determined to have made the journey.

The ward sister told the doctor about the woman who visited Sandra a few days ago. She thought her name was Sally, but she had not been back to visit again.

The doctor put the envelope in his pocket, and the two of them walked together towards the ward. Sandra was still in her own isolation room; her breathing was being controlled by a respirator and drugs were fighting the infections.

As they got to the door, another nurse called out to the ward sister, she was holding the biggest bouquet of flowers she had ever seen.

"What shall I do with these? They just arrived for Sandra."

There was a card stapled to them. It read:

"SEE YOU ON THE OTHER SIDE BITCH. Mr. G x."

They decided to put the card in the bin, and the flowers were sent to the hospital chapel.

Standing over Sandra's bed, the doctor took the letter out of his pocket. He asked the ward sister what he should do with it. It must have been important, otherwise, why would her mother have been so determined to bring it to her? Was she hoping to read it out?

They could be breaking all kinds of regulations by opening the letter, but both decided it was the right thing to do.

Sitting on the bed, he opened the envelope and began to read it to himself. Once he had finished, he handed it to the sister. She read every word slowly.

When she finished, she read it again. The two of them looked at each other in silence.

The words on the paper read:

My darling daughter,

This is the hardest thing I have ever done in my life, and I sincerely wish we could have spoken before now.

I have not been honest with you and it is the biggest regret of my life.

I have wanted to tell you that your father, the man I loved with all my heart, had been in my life until September this year.

He never forgot you; he has seen you grow up through my eyes but has also seen you from a distance.

I remember the day when you were eight years old, you came home with a new friend, Sally. That new friend is your half-sister.

I wished for many years with all my heart that I could have told you the truth, but I promised Robert that I would never tell you.

I know we have had our differences in the past, and I would ask you to find it in your heart to forgive me.

If you are reading this then there is a good chance that I may not be able to read it to you. I know I am ill. I am tired and tired of living a lie.

You will always be my daughter, and I will love you forever.

God bless you, my one and only.

All my love Mum x

Chapter 120

As the boat passed Kavos at the bottom of the island, Costas took control. Steve sat at the large table just behind the captain's seat and opened a bottle of his favourite beer. He could see the women in the galley in front of him. The two of them chatted as if they had been friends for years. The sun was getting a little lower, but the sky was still blue and there were a few light clouds building over the mainland.

Sheridan clumsily made his way along the side of the boat to where Costas sat in the pilot seat.

He was having trouble standing and held on to Costas as he began to speak.

"How fast does this thing go? All we have done is chug along. I'm sure I saw a fisherman row past. Let me have a go at driving."

Costas looked behind him at Steve and shrugged.

As they swapped places, Sheridan grabbed the wheel and turned it. The boat lurched to the left causing Costas to grab hold of the back of the seat. Steve's beer was launched from the table, and the two girls ended up on the deck of the galley.

Sheridan was laughing out loud and said, "Oops."

Costas launched into a tirade of insults, all of which were in Greek. He almost punched Sheridan as he waved his arms around.

Then he reached over to the control panel, and he reduced the speed of the boat before switching it off.

Thankfully, Mari and Cynthia were only shaken up.

Sheridan, still sitting in the seat, looked around. He could see the terror on everyone's face. He knew that he had been exceptionally stupid and began again to apologise.

Steve was surprised when Costas allowed the idiot to start the engines and gently get up to speed. The girls were clearing up bottles, glass, and cushions off the deck in the galley while Steve sat on the seat, which spanned the whole rear of the boat.

For the next twenty-five minutes, all seemed calm. Costas reluctantly joined Steve on the large comfortable rear bench seat while the ladies prepared a salad in the galley.

The water was calm enough to stop while they all ate. Sheridan seemed to have learned his lesson for a while and quietly ate his lunch sitting in the pilot seat while the others sat at the table in the galley.

After lunch, the ladies cleared away while Steve and Costas returned to the bench seat at the back of the boat.

Sheridan started the engines and let them idle to warm up. The sound of them gave Steve goosepimples.

When up to temperature, Sheridan pushed the throttle lever slowly forward, and the craft was soon running at half speed.

The next ten minutes of cruising were superb. It was when Sheridan spotted Paxos in the distance that things changed.

Steve was watching the wake of the boat behind them, the motion made him feel relaxed. Sheridan shouted at the top of his voice, "Land Ahoy!"

Steve looked forward and saw Mari standing in the galley entrance. He only saw her for a split second.

Sheridan pushed the throttle lever as far forward as he could. The engines responded with a throaty roar, and the front of the craft lifted.

Steve watched Mari as she lost her balance, and then he heard her scream.

The noise was familiar, like cutting a melon. The next few seconds happened in slow motion. The boat was going fast and hitting each wave with a loud slap. The pilot, oblivious to what was going on behind him, had one arm in the air as if he was on a rodeo horse and was whooping loudly.

The woman he loved and adored was in front of him. He could see the look of terror on her face. Her skin was white. He couldn't hear her screaming but knew she was. The only thing he could hear was the blood pumping in his head.

He looked again at Mari. She was frozen to the spot. This time he noticed what was falling from her grip.

The spear gun bounced as it hit the deck.

Steve felt calm. He didn't notice the carbon rod that had pierced his chest. The tip of it had passed right through him and the cushion behind him. It was now embedded into the thickest part of the composite shell of the hull.

Blood was seeping through his shirt and soaking his blue shorts.

He knew what had happened and was powerless to change things; the air around him smelt and tasted different, a taste he knew well.

Mari was in front of him, on her knees, still screaming silently when he coughed. He watched as she was showered in blood. She was crying out to him. As he looked at her he could sense a change. Nothing was clear; slowly his vision and the terror in front of his eyes began to fade.

He was in the room.

White walls, no ceiling, bright white; it hurt his eyes, and he was afraid to blink. The white table was below him and the white covered book sat still. He urged it to open, but the cover did not move.

He blinked and the book was gone.

I'm sure you will be intrigued to know what happens next; it's not the end!

The sequel *Dying to Live* will answer some of your questions as well as creating new ones with twists and turns along the way.

Thank you for reading and watch this space!

Russell D Whitney

Printed in Great Britain
by Amazon